Key Weirder

Robert Tacoma

Mango Press
Gainesville, Florida

For information address
Mango Press
P.O. Box 141261
Gainesville, FL 32614-1261
mangopress@gmail.com

This is a work of fiction. Names, characters, places, and incidents either are products of the author's imagination or are used fictitiously. Any resemblance to actual events or locales or persons, living or dead, is entirely coincidental.

For information on books by Robert Tacoma:
www.tacobob.com
mangopress@gmail.com

Front cover illustration by T. Jaegar and Greg Hatcher.
Back cover illustration by Greg Hatcher.
Cover and interior design by Merrey Design.

First U.S. edition published 2005

ISBN: 0-9760630-1-8

10 9 8 7 6 5 4 3 2 1

For Sara Leigh

"I don't regret nuthin'"

— Keith Richards

Key Weirder

Chapter 1

The Good Life for Taco Bob

"Maybe even a little too good."

There always seemed to be a bar upwind, no matter where I sat on the beach. This time it was Calypso music and the smell of shrimp cooking that came my way courtesy of a warm sea breeze. I tried a sip off a cold Corona, leaned back in my chair, dug my toes a little deeper into the Key West sand, and took a quick count of the fingers on my right hand. When I looked up there was sixteen-year-old Willie, wearing two baggy pairs of swim trucks and two ball caps, standing in front of me in the bright sunshine. His ebony face looked painfully bored, as usual.

"Wassup, Taco Dude? How come yer always looking at yer hand anyway?"

"Just checking on my fingers to make sure I got the right amount. It's just kind of an exercise thing I do to help me learn better dreaming."

Willie, of Two Willies Seashells, plopped himself down on the sand next to my chair.

"Uh-huh, whatever."

Young Willie's attention was momentarily diverted by a couple of teenage girls walking along the beach.

"My grandfather says for you to come by this evening for dinner. He's got some steaks or something going on."

"Tell your grandfather wild horses couldn't keep me away."

"'Kay. See ya."

Without another word Willie was on his feet and shyly following the girls down the beach at a safe distance.

* * *

I didn't always spend my afternoons lazing around tropical beaches. In fact, at one time I was your typical hard-working cowboy, running a possum ranch in Armadillo, Texas.

But life has a way of throwing changes at you about the time you least expect it. A few more than the usual amount of tornados, floods, and prairie fires coupled with some misunderstandings with the law a while back had me leaving my contented life in the Texas panhandle. I headed south, looking for a change in scenery and luck.

By the time I got to Key West I was not only out of road but out of money too. Since the place seemed to have ample quantities of outstanding weather, world-class fishing, funky bars, great food, and fine-looking women, I decided it might be worth staying put and trying to make a go of it in the Conch Republic.

I found Key West to be everything I'd hoped for and more. Thanks to an insurance windfall from the possum ranch, most days I could be found either fishing for grunts or relaxing on the beach, the beach being an excellent place for perfecting the kind of tropical lifestyle I'd been told required watching sunsets over sparkling blue-green water as much as possible. I was up for the challenge.

Life was good. Almost too good.

* * *

I took a quick swim and got cleaned up a little before I went by Willie's to see about that dinner invite. The elder Willie was sitting on the front porch with a bottle of spiced rum and two glasses. I'm usually not one to do much liquor drinking before dinnertime, but my host insisted and I decided a good snort just might hit the spot.

Mr. Willie is an old black feller who spent most of his life on the water around the Bahamas and Florida Keys before he settled into his current entrepreneurial situation as Key West's seashell man. He saved his money for years and finally bought a nice little house in town. He'd recently been breaking his young grandson Willie into the business.

A world-class grunt fisherman, Mr. Willie had taught me more about the tasty hand-sized fish than I would have ever thought there was to know.

I hadn't really had a good sit-down with the old man since coming back from a trip to the Ten Thousand Islands and Everglades National Park area. So I was looking forward to a pleasant evening in the company of a fine storyteller and friend. We sat there on his porch, with the breeze rattling the palms, and had us a drink while we waited for the charcoal on the grill to burn down.

"Taco mon, I see you catching them grunt today out on the little pier. You good. You got the patience like a old man since you come back to Key West."

I took a sip of that spicy rum and worked up a little smile.

"I did have me some further training in fishing techniques while I was off to the Everglades. I ain't told nobody else, but I met a ol' feller who was living out there in the swamp, and he let me stay with him for a while."

This got Mr. Willie's attention. He leaned forward in his rocking chair and looked me in the eye. "No shit? They somebody still living out there in the park in this day? I thought them rangers run all them squatters out from there years ago! What that man's name? What he be looking like?"

I sipped rum and told the story of Mr. Henry Small, a mysterious old man living in a little cabin way up one of the creeks in the most remote part of the Everglades National Park. I told how I had gotten sick and Mr. Small, who didn't look a day under 100, had brought me to his cabin and got me fixed up. Mr. Small had taught me some things about fishing and living in the swamp while I was staying with him. Man even had a little boat made out of a log like the Indians used to have around there.

I was about to tell Old Willie about the intensely vivid fever dreams I'd had while I was sick, but he jumped in the next time I went for a sip.

"Now that is some evermore crazy shit! They used to be a mon like what you talking about there, but he the old mon back when I was on the water them many years ago! Can not be the same one!"

Mr. Willie started to go off into some hard thinking, but a blast of really loud music coming from inside the house had him on his feet.

"Willie! You turn that damn devil music down NOW, boy! I tell you every time that music hurts the walls of this old house!"

The music volume decreased dramatically and the old man sat back down.

"That boy watch too much of that MTV! That shit going to rot the brain right from his head, I know!"

I tried not to laugh, but a little bit slipped out. Old Willie gave me a look like was I crazy, and then he got a grin going and we were both laughing as we headed around back to check on the charcoal.

* * *

Besides being an expert on seashells, sea stories, and grunts, Mr. Willie's a damn fine cook too. The man got those steaks grilled to perfection and served up with peas 'n' rice, lobster salad, johnnycakes, and bread pudding for dessert.

After we'd polished off that fine meal, we adjourned back to the front porch to have a short one before I carried it on home. Home being the little wooden camper on the back of my pickup truck, parked at a friend's house.

"What you got going on for yourself now, Taco mon? You going to be the Grunt Fisher of Key West? Or maybe sit there on the beach doing them crossword puzzles so much roots grow out you ass like a tree?"

The old man was smiling, but I knew he was serious too.

"I been giving it some thought Mr. Willie, but I ain't really come up with a definite plan just yet. Not hurting for money bad or anything, since I still got most of the insurance money from my ranch out West."

About then young Willie appeared on the porch and snapped to attention, saluted, and announced that the dishes were washed. There followed another short one-sided debate concerning the volume of the TV, and then it was quiet again. Mr. Willie looked at me and made a motion with his hands for me to proceed.

"So, I been thinking of going to Orlando and maybe seeing Mary Ann sometime. Maybe drive on up to North Carolina and do a little fishing with Pete. Other than that, I ain't come up with much."

The old man leaned back in his chair and got to rocking. "You don't act like that going to do it for you though. You need something else going on or you already be gone doing that."

He was right, of course. I didn't really know what to do with myself. A man can take only so much of a good thing. Even grunt fishing and hanging around Key West could get old after a while. I'd been seeing that as a good problem to have, but lately I'd been a bit restless.

It was my turn to give him the thing with the hands to go on. He did.

"You all the time reading them books about Florida, you can just write one too! Only about half the people living in Key West writers, plenty room for one more!" He laughed and gave me a full showing of teeth with a lot of gold before going on with what he had in mind. "I sometimes think I write a book with my recipes, but it's not happening. I tell you what, mon. You write about you going fishing around, and I give you some recipes for you to put in the book too!"

That got my attention. It took a couple more snorts of rum for us to get the details worked out, but it was the start of a plan. When I went to get up to leave, the old man put a solid grip on my shoulder.

"You go, you just be careful, mon. There plenty enough crazy shit out there on the road these days. Them Daltons you tell me about once, them's the kind of thing I mean."

I told him I wasn't too worried about the Daltons, since they'd been taking their meals inside lately, part of a long-term arrangement with the Department of Corrections. However, I didn't mention that escaping from prison was on the boys' long list of talents currently frowned upon by the criminal justice system.

* * *

The next day I did some light grunt fishing and some heavy thinking. I had a fishing spot next to the park with one scraggly ol' leaner palm for shade. Other than having to move every so often to stay in the shade, it was a mighty fine place for catching dinner and contemplating life. The old man's suggestion about traveling around and writing a book still sounded like a good idea. Not the best idea, mind you, but it was leading the pack at that point.

I got out my map and got down to serious planning. Figured just ease on around the state, fishing and cooking as I went. Make some notes along the way, then come back to Key West and write a bestseller. How hard could it be?

I decided it best to stick with trying to catch one kind of fish wherever I went. Since grunts were mostly a South Florida thing for inshore fishing, I figured I'd go with the statewide favorite: trout. *Trout Fishing in Florida* sounded like a good title for my bestseller even.

There was another reason to go, something I hadn't mentioned to Willie Sr. Just before I'd left the swamp to head back to Key West, the strange old man in the little cabin had vanished on me. I hadn't been that worried about it at the time; but the more I thought about it, the more it seemed like something just wasn't right.

Chapter 2
Julian

Not far from where Taco Bob was fishing for grunts and making plans, a young man sat down on a rock. It was late afternoon and Julian Espejo had just gotten into town. Julian sat in awe, seeing the marker for the first time. He had seen pictures, but pictures could not do justice to the magnificent concrete marker that stood just a few feet before him, with the turquoise waters of the Atlantic in the background. It was a gaudy red, black and yellow, with the words "Conch Republic — Southernmost Point, Continental USA, Key West, FL, painted on the inland side.

Julian was spellbound. The monument was nearly ten feet tall and six feet wide, and it looked like it must weigh tons.

Faintly at first, but then louder by the minute, he could hear the music from the soundtrack to one of those old Clint Eastwood westerns in his head. As a boy he had watched the videos of those westerns over and over. The throbbing music made him think of his town, his friends, his family, and his quest. When he'd left for Key West, the whole town had gathered on the dusty streets to see him off. The men and boys in their best suits, the women and young girls in their long dresses. They gave him baskets of food for his journey and sang the traditional songs of the region. He clearly remembered the emotion-choked words of his father outside the bus station as he waved good-bye.

"Julian my son, I know you have go to. It is your time. Your destiny awaits. When you return, bring us something nice, okay?"

As he stood now, transfixed before the monument, pride swelled in his chest and tears came to his eyes. The music in his head became louder and louder, until it was like a runaway locomotive. Then something shook him and he heard a voice, a high-pitched, whiney voice.

"Excuse me. EXCUSE ME!"

The music ran off the tracks and crashed. Julian wiped the tears away and stared at the portly middle-aged woman who had a sweaty grip on his arm.

"Excuse me, young man, but could you take our picture?"

The woman was sunburn pink and wearing a bright red Hawaiian shirt.

"Just look through here, and when you see the blue dot at the top, you press this. Got it?"

She waddled over to the marker and stood next to a round man wearing an identical shirt, and they both smiled big.

"Look for the blue dot!"

Julian had a little trouble with the camera, but after some further coaching by the woman, he finally got a few shots that seemed to satisfy her.

After they left he tried to get the music going in his head again, but he could only come up with the song "Tequila Breakfast." Someone sitting behind him on the bus had played the classic Marty the Manatee song on their CD player over and over all the way from Miami. The song had brought former Key West resident Marty fame and fortune and, for years since, had brought hordes of young people to the Keys to party. Julian couldn't get the song out of his head — he had lost the moment.

Julian's thoughts drifted again to his beloved hometown and its people. Brownspot was small; its people, fiercely proud. It didn't even show up on most maps, down below Brownsville in the bottom of Texas — southernmost Texas — on the border with Mexico. The town hadn't changed in years. Its people still made their living the time-honored way, as their forefathers had, by smuggling drugs and illegal aliens.

But the people of Brownspot were tired of the quiet, small-town life and hungered for the money, excitement, noise, pollution, crime, and overcrowding that could come to their community if only they had something that would literally put them on the map.

Always shy and quiet, Julian had recently turned 21 and wanted to prove himself to his family and his town. He planned to see that Brownspot got the recognition it deserved as the true Southernmost Point in the Continental USA.

Julian looked hard at the giant hunk of concrete. He hadn't come for a silly picture, he had come for much more. He had come to steal the marker.

Chapter 3
On the Road Again With Taco Bob

"Trying to keep my mind on trout."

With my flats boat on the trailer behind my old truck, I left out of Key West. It was another beautiful tropical morning, and I was fired up and looking forward to seeing what was waiting for me up the road. I'd gotten my camping and fishing supplies all sorted out the day before. I had plenty of cash, plenty of time, and an open mind. I figured I was set.

I'd stopped by the Mallory docks for the daily Sunset Celebration the evening before, looking for a friend I hadn't seen since my return from the Everglades. Ponce the Cat Juggler was nowhere to be found, though. I tried inquiring as to his whereabouts amongst the mimes, musicians, and assorted local oddballs hanging around the dock. All I got was shrugs, blank looks, and several opportunities to purchase postcards, drugs, or time-share condos.

A quick stop by the place where the sole surviving descendant of Ponce de Leon had been staying with his cats got me nothing but strange looks from the landlady. This got me to worrying, since the last time I'd seen Ponce, he was still talking about taking off and looking for a fountain of youth like all the Ponces before him had. Often with tragic results.

I decided to make a serious effort to find the man as soon as I got back from researching my upcoming bestseller.

* * *

The highway going through the Keys has gotta be one of your more scenic drives anywhere. All size islands in a row connected by bridges, over some of the most gorgeous water in the world. I guess I might've been a little sad leaving Key West, but I had every intention of coming back.

I seen a new little drive-thru place called Governor's Chicken Burritos along one lonely stretch of road and would have stopped, but it was still early and the place was closed. I remembered the time I seen a feller wearing a shower cap and a skirt run out on that same key and grab a fresh road-kill 'diller off the blacktop. I was still thinking about that when a red Corvette coming from the other direction blew by, just a gettin' it. I seen brake lights in the mirror. The 'vette did a u-turn, following along behind in the traffic. Had to be tourists.

The plan was to work my way around the state for a few days and try out some spots for trout fishing. Wanted to check out the area on the east coast of the state first, then jump on over to the panhandle and come back down the west coast. I took in all the fine scenery going on with the water every shade of blue stretching out to the horizon as I cruised over bridges thinking about trout.

There's several kinds of sea trout found in the waters around Florida, but the most popular is the Speckled Trout.

If you find yourself with a streamlined fish with a big mouth and lots of little spots on the sides, chances are it's a Speck. They're mostly inshore all along the coast of Florida, but come winter they sometimes go up the rivers looking for warmer water. Most of your trout are about one or two pounds, but they get bigger and are called gator trout. Those were the ones I was looking for.

I decided to give Miami a wide berth and head on up to the Cape Canaveral area first. There were several reasons for this. Mainly, I was driving an old pickup truck with a homemade camper on the back and pulling a boat full of gear. A city the size of Miami just didn't feel right.

The area a little further north, around the Cape, was supposed to have some of the best trout fishing in the state, so I figured why not just start with that. Playing into my decision-making process was also the fact that Mary Ann, a young woman I'd been involved with romantically in a big way in the not too distant past, had been calling and leaving messages for me at the house where I'd been parking my truck. She wanted to see me again. She was in Orlando, and Cape Canaveral was conveniently close by.

Mary Ann and me had met up in Key West not that long ago and had hit it right off. We spent some quality time together, and I was pretty well heartbroken when she all of a sudden up and left for Orlando one day. I called her the day before I headed out on my trout fishing expedition and what she had to say on the phone was weighing heavily on my decision to head for the middle of the state first. In fact, I ended up thinking more about her than trout fishing, driving up through the Keys that morning.

Chapter 4

Plotting and Planning

Julian was back after spending the night in a motel room smaller than he thought possible.

The marker for the Southernmost Point in the Continental USA was a lot bigger than it looked in the picture Julian had seen on the Internet. It was really big, and heavy. The original plan of renting a small truck and hiring a couple of men to help him load it was going to need some fine-tuning.

Walking from the motel, the radio in a passing out-of-state car had been blaring "Tequila Breakfast," so that was back in his head.

Since taking pictures of tourists every few minutes would disrupt his planning, he stood a little further back, over by the fence. Staring at the monument, he tried to concentrate. An image of the earnest townsfolk of Brownspot waving goodbye at the bus station came into his mind. Perhaps a larger truck, he thought, and even more men to help. In his mind, Julian started to hear the first few deep notes of "A Fistful of Dollars" over the "Tequila Breakfast" line about coconut trees and warm ocean breeze. Maybe some kind of mechanical lift would work. The music was getting a little clearer, he could hear the trumpet start to come in. And not just a lift, but maybe...

"Excuse me?"

Julian slowly turned to meet his next pushy, middle-aged photography instructor. The music stopped, all the music. Even the line about conch fritters and beer was finally gone from his head. Silence.

"I hate to bother you and all, but could you take a picture of my friend and me? I would really appreciate it."

This was different. Blonde, big eyes, big smile, about his age. The friend the same but with brown hair. Both very slim and very female in shorts and tank-tops.

"You just have to look through..."

Before she could finish, Julian cut in while taking the offered camera, "the viewfinder on the top and wait for the blue dot, then press this."

Big friendly smiles.

"A little closer together! That's it! This camera should be proud to take pictures of such beautiful ladies! Another? No, I don't mind at all! Let's see those smiles!"

They were from Gainesville, taking a break from school and didn't know anyone. Why didn't he meet them at a bar called Sloppy Joe's in a little while, and they'd buy him a drink for being so nice and taking their picture?

Julian watched them walk down the street toward Old Town. They walked nice. He kind of liked the blonde and would feel bad later about not meeting them at the bar. It's not that he hadn't planned to, he had. But he got an even better offer a few minutes later from a redhead from North Carolina.

Chapter 5

Mary Ann and Taco Bob

"Trout was the farthest thing from my mind."

Between the explaining and crying and holding and love-making and talking and understanding and more love-making and eating and laughing, we weren't getting much sleep that first night, so we decided not to go fishing the next morning.

I'd managed to get lost a couple of times looking for the little apartment on the outskirts of Orlando where Mary Ann was staying with another woman. By the time I found the place it was almost dark. We had some serious talking to do, so after I came in and met the roommate, Mary Ann and me sat out in the truck.

As soon as the door closed, she put her arms around my neck and looked at me with those big sad eyes. "I was such a dumbass to leave you like I did. Can you ever forgive me?"

With a woman like Mary Ann pressed up against me, it was hard not to feel forgiving. I indicated amnesty was a distinct possibility, but otherwise kept quiet. I let her sit back and tell me about her past — something she hadn't been big on doing before.

"At the ripe old age of nineteen I thought I knew a helluva lot more than I really did. I had it in my head I couldn't live without this guy I knew, so I moved in with him. That's when I found out he was a crazy control freak. So I got out of there and ended up staying with friends in LA, hiding from the whacko.

"Then I met this guy at a party, an old guy, but a real smooth talker. Turns out he wrote books on sorcery and the occult, and lived in a big mansion with a few other girls. What can I say? I went for it. Figured it would at least be a good way to lie low for a few months.

"The old guy started calling us the Witchettes and the name stuck. Eight years later I'd been with him longer than any of the others still around. A lot of girls came and went over the years, and he eventually lost interest in me. He turned into a manipulative old bastard with his little harem, always wanting new girls. But I stuck around because ... well, I'm not really sure why I stuck around."

Mary Ann started losing it a little, so it was time for me to come up with a warm hug and a cold bottle of water so she could go on with her story. Turns out the fella was Charlie Spider, head of the Spider Cult and writer of several popular New Age books, including one on dreaming that I'd read some of myself. That book explained that if you looked at your hands several times a day and purposefully counted the fingers, sooner or later you'd do it in your dreams. According to the book, when you're dreaming you'll usually have too many or too few fingers. The trick then is to realize you're having a dream and that everything going on around you is not real. This is what the book called waking up in a dream, or lucid dreaming. What all you were supposed to do next I wasn't too sure about, since I hadn't read that far in the book. I figured I better check it out soon though, because I'd found my hands in dreams a couple times lately.

I spoke up to say I was familiar with Charlie's books.

"Well, you might know he died not too long ago then. He was always so full of life and so sure of himself. We were so used to him being there and running everything, and I mean everything, and then he got sick." Mary Ann looked at me and I could see the tears shining in her eyes from the streetlight. She put her head on my shoulder as a yellow Porsche hummed slowly down the street.

"When he got sick, it was like his life was being sucked out of him a little every day. He went from this intense, dominating force to a shriveled old man in just a few days. It was awful. When he died, I just wanted to go, to get as far away as possible."

Mary Ann said when she got to Key West she was broke and got a job at the bakery there where I first seen her. She also got a job dancing at the local topless club a couple of nights a week.

She told me the night before she left town, she'd been on stage when one of the women from the Spider Cult had come in. She wasn't sure if the woman named Carol had recognized her or not because Mary Ann was wearing a long red wig over her buzzcut blonde hair. She decided she didn't want to hang around to find out why, or even if, Carol was looking for her, so she'd packed her bags the next morning, told me goodbye with little explanation, and cut town.

"I should have stood my ground, Taco. I've gone over it a thousand times since then, and there's no reason for those people to be looking for me. There's nothing they could say or do that would make me want to go back there."

Thus commenced the first serious round of hugging and crying and assuring and reassuring. She wanted us to go inside to her room, and we managed to get most of our clothes off for the next step of the reconciliation process, which didn't seem to require any talking.

* * *

Later on, while we were sitting in bed eating ice cream, I told her that the topless place there in Key West closed for a few days not long after she left. The word around town had the owner and one of the bouncers doing the mysterious disappearance thing. They'd last been seen going out in a fishing boat with a young woman and everyone right off figured mob hit because the old man had some shady friends in Miami. Rumor was the cops thought the bouncer had taken the contract to off the old man and then disappeared himself. There was some talk the feds were looking for him in Kansas, but after the bar reopened under new management with half-price drinks, people started forgetting about the whole thing.

I told Mary Ann what I was up to with fishing around the state for trout and maybe writing about it.

She stopped licking out her bowl and proudly announced, "Well I got a good job with a security consulting outfit here in Orlando, and I bought myself that nice little Toyota you saw out front."

She gave me a self-satisfied smile. I countered.

"I been working on becoming one of your better grunt fishermen down there in Key West. I'm hoping my expertise in procuring grunts is going to help me in my endeavors to catch more and bigger trout."

She give me a funny look with those big eyes.

"I'm pretty sure I can get a day off to go with you and check out your fishing skill." She then started licking out my bowl. I stretched out comfortable and leaned back on the pillows with my hands behind my head.

"You're sure welcome to come along, ma'am. In fact, you play your cards right, you might even get the opportunity to try your hand at some challenging trout fishing yourself."

She gave me a laugh and said I was as full of shit as ever, then went to get the last of the ice cream. I was lying there on the bed, working up a nice contented smile. Mary Ann came back in the bedroom and said she'd forgot to put the ice cream back in the freezer and now it was kind of runny. So we ate the hard part and started pouring the melted part on each other and laughing and licking. Things were going so well, I snuck a count of my fingers to make sure this wasn't going to turn out to be just one of my better dreams. Mary Ann saw what I was doing, grabbed me by the ears, and raised my face up to hers.

"Count your fingers if you want, but let's not talk about the Spider Cult anymore. If I never hear another word about those people it will be fine with me."

Chapter 6
Carol

Back in Los Angeles, the Spider Cult was doing better than ever. Head Witchette Carol Derriére slipped off her bed in the Spider Mansion and stretched lazily as she walked toward the window. Outside on the lawn, several of the remaining Witchettes were practicing new exercises for the Spider Cult Workshops and Seminars they gave around the world. Carol approved.

"My, that looks like a lot of work. It also looks like a lot of money, and I do love money."

Carol glided over to her desk and took another look at some calculations from their accountant. The Head Witchette had set to work making the Spider Cult as profitable as possible as soon as she recovered from her ordeal in Florida. The sales of handbooks, t-shirts, and videos from the workshops were up nicely, as were the royalties from Charlie's line of mystical self-help books. Carol smiled contentedly.

"Perhaps I should dress? A little shopping might be nice."

As busy as she was, Carol still found time to develop an appreciation for erotic, yet refined, apparel. She'd found that a strict regime of uninhibited shopping sprees to the boutiques of Rodeo Drive helped keep the stress within manageable levels.

Someone was at her bedroom door.

"Yes?"

It was Heather. Shy, quiet, unassuming, and detestably thin Heather.

"Come in, dear. What is it?"

"Someone's here. It's Charlie's nephew, Jeremy. He wants to borrow money again. I told him we didn't have any money, that you were the only —" Heather started to cry.

"Where is he now?" Carol didn't want Jeremy around the mansion because he was a sneaky little perv. There were other reasons as well.

"I think he went into the kitchen. He — he put his hands on me." Again, more tears.

"Look, Heather. You need to learn to be more assertive in these kinds of situations." Carol put a reassuring arm around the svelte blonde. No matter what Heather ate, she never gained an ounce. Carol ate one little bon-bon, and her ass swelled to the size of a dirigible.

"Go down to the kitchen, look Jeremy in the eye, and say, 'No!' Then give him a good shot in the face with this." She handed over a can of mace the size of a fire extinguisher.

Heather's face brightened. "Thanks, Carol! You always know just what to do."

Carol shooed her charge out the door and started back to her desk. She had a thought, and went to the little secret hiding place in her room.

She hadn't seen the two gold idols in a while. They felt good in her hands. They were a little something she'd found in Charlie's room soon after he'd died. No one else knew about them. No one except Jeremy.

Carol was thinking about Charlie's diary when a blood-curdling scream came from the kitchen downstairs. She smiled.

"Good work, Heather."

The idols went back in their box, and the diary came out. Carol read again of the tremendous power the Chacmools supposedly possessed. Of course there was a catch — there was one missing. The diary said that the complete set of three Chacmools was needed for the power to manifest itself. Then when the three idols were placed on the body of a person who had entered into the realm of lucid dreaming, not only would that person be able to control the dream, but the dream would become reality. There were a lot of possibilities here, not the least of which would be having control over anyone she wished. Carol hadn't mastered lucid dreaming yet, but she figured she'd cross that little bridge when she had all three Chacmools.

But she'd already struck out following the trail of the third idol to Florida with Jeremy in tow. It was days of frustration and uncomfortable associations, followed by the worst night of her life in a disabled boat in a mosquito-plagued swamp during a thunderstorm. The next day she was so out of it, she didn't pay much attention to the fisherman who rescued them. She was so sick, she didn't even notice the bag she sat on in the fisherman's boat was bruising her ass. Back at the mansion at last, she'd checked the bruise against one of the Chacmools. It was a perfect match.

Carol knew it was a long shot, but she really wanted to know what was in that bag she'd been sitting on.

As bad as she wanted that other Chacmool, Carol was staying the hell away from Florida. There were people she could hire to find this fisherman for her. Professionals who could locate him, maybe even make some inquiries about what was in that bag. He shouldn't be that hard to find. How many thin, suntanned guys with a southern drawl could be riding around the waters of south Florida in a white boat anyway?

* * *

Only the best private detective agency in LA would do, so Carol looked in the phone book and called the one with the biggest ad.

Thompson's Discreet Inquiries had their offices just off Rodeo Drive, a plus in Carol's book. An appointment was set up for that afternoon, and Carol squeezed into a tasteful bustier and designer jeans ensemble for the meet. A quick check in the mirror on the way out showed just the kind of voluptuous bod any girl could ask for, plus about five pounds. Other than the weight thing, Carol liked what she saw - a sophisticated and sexy look that demanded respect.

Two gentlemen, one of them Mr. Thompson himself, and the other, Paul Smit, head of investigations, met with her in their well-appointed offices. Except for Smit staring at her breasts, the men were polite and professional. Their ad said they specialized in delicate matters for celebrities. Another plus. Carol wasn't really a celebrity, but she liked to think of herself as one. At least she dressed the part.

"Gentlemen, you see before you a woman who needs a man." A quick wink at Smit. "But not just any man." She held up a designer checkbook. "My little friend here and I are looking for a man with a lumpy sack."

The Head Witchette wrote a check for the deposit after giving them all the information she could think of about the fisherman and his boat. Carol left her checkbook out on the table, pen in hand.

"If during the course of your investigation you should happen to find a little gold statue somewhere in the vicinity of the fisherman, I would be more than happy to pay double the normal fee."

That got their attention. There was some token mentioning of possible ethical and legal problems with such a recovery operation, but all that seemed to be resolved by Carol opening her checkbook again. They took the photograph of the Chacmool and another substantial check. When Carol left, everyone was smiling.

* * *

"Christ on a stick! You see the outfit that woman was wearing? What a slut!" Thompson continued shaking his head in disbelief as he dropped the picture of the gold figurine on the table, then started going through some furniture catalogs at the end of the conference table.

"Yes, her clothes were a bit provocative."

Thompson looked up at the younger man, who seemed on the verge of a major blush.

"Provocative? I thought you were going to drool all over the contract before she could sign it."

Smit's face went to full blush. Thompson didn't notice; he opened a catalog and flipped pages.

"Who have we got to put on this?"

Smit cleared his throat.

"We'll have to sub this out; all our people are jammed. Jim and his boys are still on the Nicholson stakeout, and Eddie's got his team on the Malone situation. Gary'll be back from vacation next week, but you know he doesn't like to work out of town."

Thompson picked up another catalog and motioned for Smit to continue.

"There's one guy that did work for us before, out of Georgia. A bounty hunter named Saul Thorpe. Big guy with a shaved head and tattoos, he's not what you'd call a class act. Been in trouble a few times for being a little too aggressive in his investigations. He's cheap though."

"Sounds like our man. Make it happen." Thompson held a catalog up, "Which of these wall coverings do you like for the lounge, the beige or the tan?"

Chapter 7

Saul

Saul stuck to the back roads as much as possible. When he was driving on a country road, he tried to keep from having cars too close in front or behind him. He liked to have some room.

He liked the narrow two-lane roads for one of his hobbies motorcycles. He hated motorcycles. He hated a lot of things, but hating motorcycles could be good sport.

The only time Saul chewed gum was while he was driving. Nothing like cruising along in the van doing sixty, a big wad of gum going, and seeing a bike coming toward him up ahead. Check the back quick. Form the gum into a perfect ball, and spit it in his hand. Ready.

A good lob with just the right wrist action and a little luck would give the biker a wad in the face at 120 mph. Nothing like it to break the monotony of driving. Kept you alert.

Saul had experimented with different projectiles. D-cell flashlight batteries were awesome, as were nails and machine screws. Once, when he was really bored and a little drunk, he bought a dozen live mice from a pet store. Distributed them one at a time through a large pack of bikers coming back from a rally. Couple of great wrecks that day. Had to ditch the car after that. It was stolen anyway.

* * *

The agency said the guy he was looking for had been seen at some place on the lower west coast of Florida. So he was driving the back roads down the east coast of the state. It wasn't the fastest way, but there were usually a lot of bikers around Daytona. Then he could cut across to the west coast.

He'd been to Florida for work before. One time he was looking for this Mexican guy, jumped bail on a weapons charge. Went to the brother's house, asked where the jumper was. Guy said he didn't know, but his eyes said he was lying. Florida has these ants that make mounds a foot high out in the fields. Fire ants. Staked the brother out on one of the mounds. Guy went crazy. Ropes were cutting his wrists and ankles. Bit through the gag and his tongue. Way too much blood and noise. Turned out the guy didn't know after all.

Chapter 8

Julian

The redhead was nineteen and had come to Key West with her mother to visit Uncle Rob. They had rented a small two-bedroom house in one of the nicer compounds with a pool and hot tub. A few days before their two-week stay was over, mom had to fly back to North Carolina for some kind of emergency at work. She reluctantly agreed to let her daughter stay. After all, the rent was already paid and the uncle was around if there were any problems.

The girl with the long red hair had just come back from seeing her mother off at the airport and was taking a walk when she found Julian. She brought him back to the compound with her.

Two days later Julian was lying out by the pool in the new swim trunks the girl had bought him. She had bought him a lot of things, mostly clothes. They ate in some nice restaurants too. Mom had left her gold card for emergencies. This quiet, good-looking young man was an emergency if ever she had seen one.

* * *

Julian enjoyed the feel of the afternoon sun on his body as he lay on the pool deck with his feet dangling in the water. There was a little soreness from his times with the athletic and affectionate young woman, but it was a good soreness. He smiled.

Something blocked the sun, and he opened his eyes. His new friend and lover was standing over him.

"Hey, Uncle Rob called and said he's going to take us out on his big boat tomorrow to do some fishing. Cool, huh?"

She jumped into the pool, splashing him with water. He took his sunglasses off, laid them on the pool deck, and slipped into the water, still smiling.

* * *

Uncle Rob got all excited about the big sailfish, but Julian thought all the fish they caught were pretty amazing. He hadn't realized how colorful some of the fish like dolphin really were. It was a beautiful calm day out on the water and they were back in before it got too hot.

Uncle Rob dropped off some of the dolphin fillets at a restaurant on his way home so his favorite niece and her friend could be assured of having the freshest fish that evening.

All the sun out on the boat must have made the red-haired girl feel even more affectionate because she insisted they go have a little lie-down before getting cleaned up for dinner.

* * *

The owner of the restaurant was a friend of Uncle Rob's, and he made sure they had the best table by a window up front. The fish was excellent, broiled and served on angel hair pasta with white sauce, conch salad, and a nice bottle of French wine. After a generous slice of key lime pie, they took a stroll down lively Duval Street, then sat in on some live music at a bar with a name neither of them could remember the next day. The place was nearly empty, and they sat at a little table by the stage. The musician was a popular local singer and guitar player. He asked them if they had any songs they would like to hear. Julian didn't miss a beat.

"Anything but 'Tequila Breakfast'!"

This got a big smile from the music man.

"And you, miss? Is there something you'd like to hear?"

"How about a ballad? One with beaches and boat drinks, blue sky days and warm, romantic nights?"

"How about this?"

Neither of them had ever heard the song before, but it was lovely and sad and brought tears to their eyes. It was a new song, one he had just written. After a couple more of his own songs, the musician took a break. He sat at their table and let them buy him a beer, then told some great jokes about pirates and treasure. After a while he said he had to get back to work because the bar was filling up.

A table of people with sunburned faces begged to hear the song that had brought them to the Keys. The musician looked over at Julian and the young woman with the red hair, smiled, and shrugged his shoulders. As they made their way out of the bar, they could hear him singing the words to the familiar song.

"Tired of the snow,

But I know which way to go.

There's a place called the Florida Keys.

Gotta head down south,
and put a drink in my mouth.
Give me coconut trees and a warm ocean breeze.
Won't have to go very far,
Once I get to Sloppy's Bar.
Gotta do it all just once before I die.
All that clear blue water is near,
I could live on conch fritters and beer.
Tequila for breakfast? Think I'll give it a try!"

It was such a beautiful evening, they walked to the beach for a stroll in the cool night air. Between the two of them they could name six star constellations, then they started making up new ones. She seemed to have an endless supply of funny names for stars, and they were still laughing in the cab on the way back to the little house.

Chapter 9

Keep on Truckin'

Julian hadn't forgotten why he was in Key West, but he hadn't given it a whole lot of thought recently either. The girl with the long red hair was gone. They'd said their tearful goodbyes at the airport earlier.

But the Southernmost Monument was still there. Still massive, solid, and maybe even heavier, at least it looked heavier. It was dark and the wind was picking up. A storm was coming in, not many people out.

Julian stood back by the fence and stared at the marker in the dark. He thought about why he had come. His town, his family. He heard the opening bar from "The Good, the Bad, and the Ugly" in his head. The wind picked up.

"Excuse me."

A male voice. Julian turned slowly and was confronted by a big man with a big belly and a hat that said something about truckers doing something better.

"You wanna make twenty bucks, kid? All ya gotta do is watch my truck for an hour while I get a quick beer over at the titty bar."

The wind was making so much noise in the palm trees, Julian hadn't heard the big semi-trailer rig pull up on the street. It had a low trailer carrying the biggest yellow front-end loader he had ever seen.

"Maybe I'll pull up here a little so I ain't blocking that driveway back there. I'll leave it running for the air conditioning. Here's the key to the door in case the cops give ya a hard time about it being parked there. You know how to drive one of these? Good. I'm just going to walk over to the titty bar and have a couple of beers and be right back. Here's ten now, and there's another ten when I get back."

Julian stood there with the ten-spot in his hand, flapping in the breeze. The man swaggered down the street in the direction of the Pink Snapper. Julian could hear every note of "The Good, the Bad, and the Ugly" like he was standing in the middle of a full orchestra.

* * *

When business was good, Julian's father rented big trucks to haul illegal immigrants and/or drugs up north. Julian knew how to drive big trucks.

The loader was a different story, but it turned out to be easier than he thought. Except for a couple of palm trees and part of the fence, he had no problem getting the monument on the trailer.

The storm was getting closer and the wind was really whipping the tarp, but he finally got the marker mostly covered. It was lying down on the trailer at an angle — along with a lot of beach sand — but it was on there.

He parked the loader and put the mass of keys from the trucker in his pocket before wiping down the steering wheel and controls with a rag. He grabbed his bag and ran to the truck. The first key he tried opened the door, and he was just pulling onto the road when the rain started.

* * *

The trucker figured it wasn't his fault. If there hadn't been half-price drinks, he wouldn't have gotten so drunk. If he hadn't gotten so drunk, he would have kicked that bouncer's ass. If he'd kicked the bouncer's ass, he might have gotten out of the bar before the cops showed and hauled him off to jail.

He hoped that kid had enough sense to turn off the truck engine sometime during the night so it wouldn't use too much fuel. He needed to get one of the cops to go by and check on his truck.

Chapter 10

Indian River Trout for Taco Bob

"Trout, at last!"

The sky was just getting light as we headed east toward the coast. We stopped at a little bait place on the way for coffee. There was a friendly old fella running the place, said he used to do a little guiding. He sold us a map and marked some spots we might try for trout on the Indian and Banana Rivers.

Those rivers are long, wide, mostly shallow stretches of water running along just inland of the east coast. The Banana River sounded best, so that's where we headed.

The sun was up good by the time we got to the boat ramp. It was a fine, clear, cool morning, and it felt damn good to be running across the water with Mary Ann beside me in the boat again. There weren't many houses along the river, but plenty of bird life. We even saw a couple of eagles circling the river looking for breakfast. I stopped a couple of places and threw the cast net and pretty soon had some nice little finger mullet for bait. When we came up on some oyster bars along the mangrove shoreline, I decided to let the boat drift.

"We'll try this a while, see if there's any ornery trout here wanting to take a swat at one of our lures."

Mary Ann had been out fishing with me a couple of times down in Key West, and she was determined to show me she could hold her own fishing for trout. She stood on the bow deck casting a topwater plug while I got a pole baited up with a finger mullet to let drift behind the boat. She had a good hit on the surface, but the fish missed. She kept at it though, determined as ever.

"Taco, I've been meaning to ask you. What happened to those two guys you said were following you when you came to Key West?"

"That would be the Daltons. They got themselves caught stealing books out of the Hemingway House while I was off to the 'Glades."

"So they're in jail? You never did talk much about it, but I got the feeling those guys weren't looking out for your best interests." She turned around and gave me a look that strongly suggested I come clean.

"Lenny and George followed me to Florida after taking kind of an unauthorized leave of absence from prison. Had it in their thick heads their time behind bars was my fault, since I was on the jury found 'em guilty of breaking into damn near every house and business in a three-county area."

I was casting a jig and trying to keep an eye on the little mullet with the float out behind the boat.

"You're saying they escaped from prison and followed you to Florida? You never told me that part. You just said if I saw a little guy and a really big guy to stay away from them and let you know." My fishing partner was looking a little pissed. "But they're in jail in Key West now, nothing to worry about, end of story?"

"Well, they did slip away and stop by once after I got back in town. But the police gathered 'em up, and the last I heard they were in that big prison over by Miami."

"They broke out of jail again and 'stopped by'?" She had her sunglasses off and was giving me the narrowed eyes thing. I hate that. "You want to tell me just what that was all about?"

As a matter of fact, I didn't.

"It wasn't much. The police showed before anything happened."

"What were they planning to do? Did they have a gun or something?"

"No, no gun."

Luckily, I didn't have to explain it was more like a missile, though small as missiles go, because Mary Ann got a big strike right then that missed. That put her mind back on the things at hand.

"I can't believe another fish missed my lure! Come back, fishy. Third time's the charm!"

"Keep at it, maybe he'll give it another try."

Mary Ann was getting better at handling a rod and reel. She worked that plug slow like she knew what she was doing. Her blonde hair had grown out of the buzzcut a little, but it was still pretty short. We both had on sweatshirts for the ride out, but the sun warmed things up fast and we started shedding clothes.

"But these Daltons, they're safely locked up now?"

"Yep. I'm pretty sure we've heard the last of the Daltons."

While mulling over that pleasant thought, I tied into a nice fish and after a good fight had myself a 20-inch redfish up to the boat. I got the hook out and dropped him back in the water. Redfish are a fine eating fish, but we'd come for trout. I gave Mary Ann a big grin like I was hot stuff for catching the first fish, and she give me the finger and kept on casting.

There wasn't much else going on there, so we ran the boat up to another spot a little closer to some mangroves. We'd seen a couple of other boats earlier, and except for the occasional helicopter, it was pretty quiet out on the water.

I put the little mullet out the back of the boat with a float again and got a nice redfish on my first cast with a plug. From what I could tell, it looked like Mary Ann was doing everything right but hadn't put a fish in the boat. She wasn't saying much, just fishing. The live-bait pole picked up some floating seagrass, so I was pulling it in when Mary Ann's reel started making noise and she was fighting a fish. It took her a while, but she finally got a redfish bigger than mine up to the boat for the net. I told her I'd take her picture with the fish, so she pulled off clothes until she was down to a bikini swimsuit. I got a few pictures of the sleek, copper-colored fish and the sleek woman with the ample chest holding it, before the big red went back in the water. Mary Ann stuck her tongue out at me and went back to fishing with a satisfied smile on her face.

I was thinking maybe I should try going around the state fishing for redfish instead of trout when Mary Ann hooked into another nice red. She handled that fish like a pro and even insisted on netting it herself. This time after releasing the fish she give me the tongue thing again and then turned around and shook her ass at me a little. She gave me a real innocent look and big grin before going back to fishing, all proud of herself.

"You know this ain't fair, woman. I'm back here keeping a lookout on this other pole and watching we don't drift up on a snag or get attacked by fisherman-eating manatees or anything. Besides, that swimsuit is mighty distracting for a poor but honest fisherman like myself."

I heard a splash behind the boat and turned to see if something was after the little mullet. The bait was fine though, and when I looked back up front Mary Ann had taken the top of her bikini off so it wouldn't distract me.

"Better?"

She was giving me the innocent thing again and I gave her a nervous smile and started keeping a lookout for other boats.

I got a small shark on the pole out back and then we tried another spot. I'd managed to talk Mary Ann into putting her top back on, but every time a helicopter or another boat was anywhere near, she'd make like she was about to take it off again, just to mess with me.

Toward noon we finally started getting into some small trout. I was rooting around in the icebox for a drink when the pole out back got hit. Mary Ann grabbed it and started fighting the fish. The fish came up and thrashed the surface a couple of times like big trout do, and sure enough it was a nice gator trout. She worked him with the rod tip up high when she got him close, and then the fish made a hard run under the boat. Mary Ann let the rod tip down to the water, so he wouldn't break the line, and slowly pulled the fish back out, and I slipped the net under him. I dropped the netted trout in the boat, and Mary Ann and me high-fived and hugged. Looked to be close to a five-pound fish. After a couple more pictures the fish went on ice so he could join us for dinner later on.

We could see a few dark clouds forming to the west, so after a little more fishing, we took the scenic route back to the boat ramp.

* * *

Baked Trout with Mushroom Sauce

2 nice big skinned Speckled Trout fillets
(This is better if you catch the fish yourself, better yet if your ladyfriend catches it.)
1/4 cup rum
1/2 cup fresh lime juice
1 can condensed mushroom soup
1/2 cup milk
1 cup sliced fresh mushrooms
2 onions, sliced into thin rings
2 tsp dried oregano
2 Tbl butter
1 Tbl Old Bay Seasoning
1 handful parmesan cheese
Salt and pepper to taste

Place the fish fillets in a big baking dish coated with butter.

If you somehow forgot to buy a lime when you stopped at the store on the way back from fishing, then don't bother with the marinating and just drink the rum.

Mix the milk and mushroom soup and pour over fillets.

Put the sliced mushrooms, onion, and whatever else is left on next.

Sprinkle cheese on top of the whole thing last.

Put in a preheated oven for about 20 or 30 minutes at 350 degrees, and don't wander off and start watching the game on TV or anything.

When the fish flakes easily with a fork, it's done!

Chapter 11

The Road

Julian stuck to the back roads because he figured they'd be watching the big highways going up through the state. He hadn't stopped while coming up the Keys on the lone road to the mainland. Once he got on the mainland, he knew he had a better chance of pulling it off.

He was pumped. Julian still couldn't believe he actually had the monument. It was a long haul though, a long way to Texas.

The first gas stop in Homestead took most of his money. He called home and woke his father, who started crying when Julian told him he had the monument. His father said he'd wire money in the morning, when the Western Union office in Brownspot opened.

Julian drove up the east coast and made Daytona by morning. There was a motel outside of town where he could park the truck off the road and hitchhike into town. He found the Western Union office, and by mid-morning he was back at the motel to get some sleep. He was tired but so wound up, he lay on the bed for a long time looking at the ceiling. The music in his head became longer and slower until he was asleep.

Chapter 12

TV News for Taco Bob

"Amazingly, there was nothing on about trout."

"TB! You gotta see this!"

I came out of the bathroom into the kitchen where Mary Ann and her roommate were making breakfast and watching a small TV. I saw just the end of a report about something that happened in Key West.

"You missed it! Remember that huge concrete thing down there? The one that was supposed to be the marker for the Southernmost Point in the country? Somebody stole the sucker last night!"

They had another news update at the top of the hour while we were finishing breakfast. Sure enough, there were pictures of a big front-end loader sitting where the monument used to be. A semi tractor-trailer was missing too. The cops weren't saying much, but the news reporter said the word on the street had it a mob thing.

"The biggest thing to happen in Key West in years and I missed it!" That got me a pop in the arm from Mary Ann, but I quickly covered. “But of course, I’d rather be here with you, sugarplum darling!”

I lit up my best grin and aimed it at Mary Ann. I was watching for another jab in the arm and didn’t even think about getting kicked under the table until it was too late.

* * *

Neither one of us was real happy about me leaving, but Mary Ann had to go back to work and I had more trout to catch. After a good round of hugs and promises, I headed north up along the east coast toward St. Augustine.

Chapter 13

Task Force

After making a few discreet phone calls to make sure it really wasn't a mob thing, the Governor of Florida called a press conference to announce that he was appointing a special task force to find the stolen monument. Operation Justifiable Outrage would be a combined effort of all state and local law enforcement agencies. All major highways in the state would be monitored by air as well as on the ground. The Governor said he was considering asking Washington for additional air support.

With a fierce look in his eye, the Governor pounded his fist on the podium and glared at the reporters and cameras.

"The people of the great state of Florida will not stand still for this kind of flagrant disrespect for the law! I have been assured by my newly appointed task force commander that all our law-enforcement resources will be in place by this very evening. This matter can and will be brought to a quick and definitive resolution!"

His aides were ecstatic. They saw some great sound bites here that could be used in the upcoming re-election campaign.

Governor Walker had been an amazingly energetic and charismatic gubernatorial candidate, but he seemed to slip into a near-comatose state once in office. His tepid and lackluster style soon earned him the name Governor Sleepwalker. With another election coming up, the Governor was finally starting to show signs of his old campaign spirit. His aides couldn't have been more relieved.

Chapter 14

A Near Miss for Taco Bob

"That got my attention!"

I stuck to the back roads heading east because I wasn't in any hurry, and you tend to see more interesting stuff that way too. Once I found the Atlantic coast, I headed north along A1A for the ride up to St. Augustine. I'd called One Eyed Pete up in North Carolina before I left Key West, and again from Mary Ann's place the night before. Pete worked for me out in Texas at the possum ranch. We met up again in Key West and spent some quality time fishing together. He was going to drive down from NC and meet me in St. Augustine so we could see about finding some trout that might want to go for a ride in my boat.

Going along the coast like that, I finally couldn't stand looking out at all that Atlantic Ocean any longer and had to stop. I found a place to park my rig and walked out on the beach, took off my shoes, and stood in the surf making a few casts with my fishing pole. There were a few people walking along the beach and a couple of those small planes pulling ad banners and one with no banner that kept flying over low. Since the fish weren't interested in what I was doing and it was such a nice day, I decided to take a little stroll myself before getting back on the road.

* * *

Just after I cleared Daytona, a semi carrying something big covered with a tarp pulled out on the road from a little motel like he didn't even see me. I laid on the horn and went off the road a little. The guy swerved back and let me by, then came in behind me. All I could think of was where the hell was a cop when you needed one.

Chapter 15

A Cop

Officer Muldoon had just come on duty after attending a briefing about a stolen truck carrying a big concrete marker from Key West. Three years ago he'd been in Key West and seen the marker himself. Some people will steal anything.

He was working the section of the county north of Daytona when he saw a semi tractor-trailer come close to running a pickup with a boat off the road. He gave his motorcycle some throttle to get a closer look at the semi.

Chapter 16

Julian

Julian was awake now. That was a close call with the pickup; he didn't even notice it when he pulled onto the road. He'd only gotten a couple hours sleep before waking up and deciding to go for it.

He was cool now. Just going to follow this pickup and boat along the coast here. Not much traffic, just a motorcycle behind him.

Chapter 17
Saul

Saul was trying to keep an eye on the beach as he drove. Never know when there might be something there he needed to get a look at. Nice pair of tanned female ass-cheeks sticking out of a thong would be nice.

Had a good wad of gum going — always ready. Pickup with a boat, then a semi coming. Saul spit the gum in his hand and lobbed it at the last second. He almost hadn't seen the bike behind the big truck.

Saul watched his rearview mirror. He grinned when he saw the motorcycle go down. He was good, no doubt about it. Only bad thing was, it looked like a cop. Okay, it was a cop. Needed to try not to do that, since they were supposed to be on the same side and all.

There was a row of deep cuts along the plastic dash-board of the van. Saul pulled out a big Rambo knife and chopped in another notch. Still smiling.

Chapter 18

One Eyed Pete and Taco Bob

"Screw the trout!"

There were still a couple of hours of daylight left when I pulled into St. Augustine. Pete had made reservations for us a couple days earlier at a motel right there by the big marina.

I got myself squared away with the room and wandered on over toward the marina to wait for the man to show. There was a nice little bar and grill, where you could sit at a table and look out over the goings-on at the marina.

I talked myself into sitting there and having a little drink, since it looked like an ideal place to kick back and pass judgment on the world at large. A nice young waitress showed up and said she'd be glad to bring me any kind of drink I could think of, so I thought one up real quick and settled in.

It was an easy kind of evening to enjoy from where I was looking at life, and I was checking my hands and about done with my drink when I spotted a familiar-looking fella with an eye patch.

Pete and me done all the hand shaking and grinning, then got down to giving our opinions about the current and near-future weather. We ordered up a round of refreshments while talking fishing and life in general.

The man had him a sweet deal going up there in North Carolina alright. The fella he was working for was a big-time developer and one of your better fisherman. Turns out the man had plenty of money and was a helluva nice guy to work for, a combination Pete highly recommended. He was taking care of one of the man's boats while learning all he could about fishing, and was having a damn good time doing it.

The cute little gal brought our drinks, and we each took a good taste. Pete leaned back in his chair, crossed his arms, and came up with a mischievous grin.

"I know you're wanting to take your boat out in the morning and try for some trout, but I got something you might want to think about while we're still in the early planning stages of our fishing trip."

Since I considered myself to be an open-minded person in life's more pressing matters like drinking, fishing, and sex, I gave him the eyebrows-up signal to continue.

"There's a charter boat captain here named Captain Ron who's supposed to be one of the best for offshore in the state. The man I work for said he'd be glad to pay for a full-day charter if I wanted, said it would be good experience for me."

This sounded pretty damn good, and after some token resistance, I let myself be talked into it. Turns out Pete already had it all set up for in the morning, so it looked like the trout in the area were going to have to find somebody else to catch 'em. We sat there and talked and planned and laughed. We watched the lights come on in the marina as darkness slipped in and did its best to cover the mistakes of daylight once again.

After a fine dinner in a restaurant there by the marina, we sat out by the pool at the motel and had a short one before hitting the sack. There were fish to catch in the morning.

* * *

The next day, Captain Ron had a couple of eager fishermen on his hands at sunrise. The boat was a 27-foot Proline set up for one thing - fishing offshore. Everything on that boat was first-class equipment and was set up to take up as little space as possible. The Captain went over safety and emergency procedures with us and showed us some things about the marine radio and operating the boat. The weather looked like it was going to hold on as predicted, and we were stoked coming out of the marina, heading into the sun. There were a few other boats heading out and one seemed to be following us. I was informed it wasn't unusual for a boat to tag along hoping to find some of Captain Ron's secret spots.

When asked what kind of fish we'd like to be airing out on such a nice-looking day, I thought about mentioning the trout thing, but said we'd be proud to have a look at whatever presented itself. After a while, lines went out for trolling to see if there were any fish hanging by a weedline that we came up on. Pete and I assured Captain Ron we were both experienced seamen and could probably at least steer the boat without screwing up too bad, so he had us taking turns at the wheel while he checked the lines.

That boat was laid out so everything was right within easy reach, and Captain Ron was doing everything with no wasted movements. The man knew his stuff.

Wasn't long before we were into some small dolphin. We released 'em as they came in, and then Pete got something big really smoking the line off his reel. After getting the other lines in, we came around and ol' Pete got down to business with bringing in his fish. We figured a big kingfish and we weren't far off, as he brought up the first wahoo I'd seen. We got a quick picture of about five foot of fish with some serious teeth and about six foot of one-eyed fisherman grinning some teeth himself.

After we turned Pete's big wahoo loose, we trolled over in some deeper water and, sure enough, tied into a nice sailfish long enough to get him to jump for one quick look.

Later on Captain Ron set us up to drift over an old wreck he knew about. He rigged a couple of poles for us to bottom fish, and we sent down some baits to see what was down there. The captain was watching the electronic fish-finder and saying something about coming up on the spot when I heard Pete grunting. I looked over and seen his pole bent over hard, and he was doing his best not to get pulled overboard.

"Pete, you think you might have a bite there?"

I was grinning when all of a sudden I was in the same situation. Something mighty strong was trying to take that nice rod and reel out of my hands, and it was all I could do to hold on, pressed up against the side of the boat.

Pete finally started making some headway, and Captain Ron gaffed the big grouper, then dropped him in the boat. It wasn't pretty, but I somehow got my fish up off the bottom and he eventually joined Pete's fish there on the deck. We took a couple more pictures, dropped the big groupers on ice, and decided to head back in.

* * *

Trout Stew

2 pounds trout, or in a pinch you can substitute some nice big grouper fillets
2 Tbl butter
A good shot or two of hot sauce
Juice of one large lemon or lime
One big onion, sliced
4 potatoes sliced
Salt and pepper to taste

Place cleaned fish fillets in cooking pot and almost cover with water. Add potatoes, salt, pepper, butter, hot sauce, and lemon juice. Place onions on top and cook over medium heat until fish is tender.

Don't wander off looking at the women by the pool or anything because if you cook this too long, the fish pieces will fall apart. Mighty fine meal for two hungry people!

Chapter 19

Chokoloskee

Chok wasn't much as far as Saul could tell. A little island down at the end of a causeway off the southwestern part of the state. A few houses and motels, some fish camps, and a marina with some boats. Not Saul's kind of place. No action.

He pulled out the information folder from the agency out in LA. Tall, thin, middle-aged guy with a hat and a southern drawl in a white boat, probably a flats boat. Great. Saul had seen two or three guys made that just driving in. If he could find this fisherman, all he had to do was call it in and get paid. But if he found the guy, he'd damn sure ask him about this little gold statue called a Chacmool he had a picture of. Maybe get paid double.

Went over to the marina and found some big sunburned stiff with a mustache. Guy was pumping gas into a boat at the dock.

"You work here, sport?"

The mustache looked up. Pretty big guy, alright.

"Yes sir, can I help you?"

Saul figured he could take him. Guy like this usually went down easy if you hit hard when he wasn't expecting it.

"Yeah, you can help me. I'm looking for a guy. Middle-age, tan, thin, fishing hat, talks southern, in a white flats boat."

Mustache got the joke, started smiling. Saul had more.

"Dropped off a couple of people here a while back. Man and a woman with a busted boat. He pulled them in."

Smiling time was over, light clicked on in mustache's head.

"You might mean the same ones the cops were asking about. The couple got a ride out of Chok with a trucker and left the boat. Guy from Key West came and claimed the boat the day after the cops were here, hauled it off. The fisherman that dropped 'em off, he got gas and left. Hadn't ever seen him around before, don't know who he was. Must have been from down south, maybe Flamingo or the Keys."

Not good. Saul needed more than this.

"You see the guy? See his boat?"

Mustache had to think about this.

"You don't look like you're with the cops."

Saul got a lot of this.

"No, I'm with the Girl Scouts. This guy stiffed a little girl on a box of cookies and I'm here to bring him to justice."

Saul flipped out his official-looking PI license in its special holder, letting his shirt come up so mustache could see the gun stuck in his waistband. The license was currently suspended, but Saul figured the gun more than made up for that little detail.

Everyone was smiling now, everyone wanted to cooperate.

"Seems like he was clean shaven, a little weathered looking. Thin guy like you said, had on sunglasses and a hat, don't remember much else about what he looked like. Had a nice boat though. Hewes, about 18-footer, big Mercury outboard, poling platform. Maybe two, three years old."

"What about the other boat, the one from Key West?"

"I think it might have been a rental. Maybe 20 foot or so with a Yamaha. Just a flat bottom skiff, maybe a Carolina."

"Thanks, citizen, you've been a moderate help. We'll be in touch if we need anything else."

Saul gave the guy a big wink and slipped on his wraparound shades. He decided the guy was probably giving up what he had, and pistol-whipping him wouldn't be worth the trouble. Too bad.

Chapter 20
Governor

Governor Walker called another press conference after being briefed on the motorcycle cop in the hospital. The cop had a broken leg and minor injuries after being struck with an as-yet-unknown projectile while pursuing a suspect truck.

This latest development had been leaked to the press an hour before the news conference. It was a slow news day and the press was eating it up. All day there had been reports across the state of possible sightings of the missing monument and truck. Several trucks matching the description had been spotted. Numerous roadblocks and high-speed and low-speed chases had netted three separate pieces of concrete sewer pipe, a manatee sculpture headed for the Tampa Zoo, and a vintage Volkswagen on its way to Tallahassee for restoring.

The Governor appeared close to tears, but his gaze was unwavering and his head high as he extended a personal plea to each of the citizens of the great state of Florida.

"Please help our brave law enforcement officers bring these dangerous thieves to justice! We must return the monument to its rightful place so that our children, and children for generations to come will always know just where the Southernmost Point in the US is located!"

The Governor's aides were jumping up and down and high-fiving each other. That evening the communications center for Operation Justifiable Outrage was swamped with calls from the toll-free number across the bottom of the picture of the emotional Governor. Someone offered a reward and the calls doubled.

Chapter 21

Georgia Peach

Julian headed north into Georgia and got lost just above the Florida state line on a series of little back roads where the rusty street signs were shot so full of holes he couldn't read the numbers. It was almost dark when he pulled into the front yard of a little house-trailer to ask directions. He got out of the truck and realized how tired he was. An old hound dog came up to him and just stood there, so Julian scratched the dog's head.

"I reckon you ain't too bad if Duke ain't gonna bark at ya."

Julian looked up at a figure standing there on the front steps of the trailer under a lone lightbulb. It was an attractive young woman in cut-off shorts holding a toddler in one arm and a shotgun in the other.

"Come on over here fella and let me get a look at you."

Julian smiled and walked over to the light, with Duke following and giving him a few sniffs for good measure.

"My name's Julian and I'm just a little lost. I was hoping you could tell me how to get back on the road to Valdosta."

Julian got within a few feet of the young woman and stopped. She smiled a little and lowered the shotgun.

"Well, Duke seems to think you're alright, and you look mighty fine to me. Come on in I guess, and I'll get you something to eat."

Julian hadn't eaten all day. He had seconds on the fried catfish, okra, and cornbread while he learned her name was Cindy and her husband was going to be out for a while.

"My husband got him a deal for free room and board up at the state penitentiary for the next few years. While little Jessie here was still in the oven, my dear husband decided he needed money for a new truck to impress his new girlfriend, slut gal named Sharon working at the bank.

"They worked out some kinda scam to rob the bank, and of course got their thieving asses caught. She testified against him at the trial. Serves him right."

Cindy sighed and said she always fell for the bad boys.

Since Julian was looking a little tired, she told him he could take a shower and lie down on her bed for a while if he wanted. Cindy had the baby tucked away in his crib and was tucking Julian in and said maybe she'd just lie down there a little while too.

She sighed and said she bet Julian was up to something real bad. She could just tell.

Chapter 22

Back in LA

Carol knew something was wrong as soon as she went into her room at the mansion. Someone had been in there. She went straight to her hiding place and pulled out the box holding the Chacmools. Carol felt a bad pain in the pit of her stomach when she opened the empty box. She sat on the bed and cried a little. Two-thirds of the way to having anyone or anything she wanted. Gone.

Carol pulled herself together, and her grief slowly turned to rage. There was only one person in LA who even knew about the Chacmools, let alone that she had two of them.

Carol threw some things in a bag, then stopped at a twenty-four hour drugstore on the way to pay Jeremy a little visit.

Chapter 23

The Last Chance Trailer Park

It was after midnight when Carol slipped into Jeremy's house trailer just outside LA. As always, she was dressed impeccably for the occasion. Black lace teddy and black fishnet stockings with matching cape to go with her black hair and accent her tall, almost too curvy figure. Carol was hot. She was also extremely pissed.

With a black zippered bag in her hand, a riding crop under her arm, and a big diver's knife strapped to her leg, she moved purposefully through the cramped trailer.

Dirty socks and long-unwashed dishes were the predominate odors. The only light came from the bedroom, so Carol moved quietly and had a look.

It was kind of cute the way Jeremy was propped up in bed fast asleep, snoring with his mouth open and a line of drool running down to his dirty undershirt. He had an empty beer can in one hand, his other hand under the spotted sheet down between his legs. The television screen was the only light in the room. It was all snow from where a videotape had run out. Carol ejected the tape — Chicks with Dicks #6.

Carol spent a moment taking in the sight of the nephew of the man once thought to hold the key to the Knowledge of the Ancient Shamans of Mexico, then went to work. She opened the bag she'd brought and laid things out on the floor, including a pair of heavy rubber gloves.

She slipped a pair of handcuffs on each of his wrists and carefully locked Jeremy's arms to the headboard. He was starting to come around, so Carol quickly pulled the sheet off and tied each ankle to a bedpost, leaving Jeremy spread-eagled and sputtering awake.

"Fuck is going on? Carol, what the fuck are you doing?"

Carol could see Jeremy was going to be a bother with this line of questioning, and she wasn't ready for him to be talking just yet. Maybe a good one to the forehead with the heavy flashlight to knock him out.

"Ouch! Jesus H Fucking Christ! Fuck that hurt! Stop that shit, Carol!"

Carol couldn't believe he didn't go out; it always worked in the movies. She gave him a couple more pops with the flashlight.

"Ow! Stop that shit! Ow! Stop it, Carol; that hurts!"

Little bastard sure had a hard head. Carol was momentarily perplexed.

"Well, then, hold still while I put this tape on your mouth, or you'll get more of the same!"

Jeremy immediately shut up and Carol slapped a piece of duct tape across his mouth. She couldn't help but notice this version of Jeremy didn't come with any pants, just an undershirt. She stood at the foot of the bed and took a little poke at Jeremy's pubes with the end of her whip.

"What's this supposed to be? Looks like something really small and furry crawled up there and died. Smells like it too."

Carol made a face, and Jeremy started to sweat and wiggle around. He was trying to say something behind the tape.

"What's the matter cretin, gotta go pee-pee?"

She gave a concerned look, and Jeremy started nodding his head and moaning.

"Well, you should have thought of that before we left the house, young man!"

Carol brought her leg up and slowly pulled the knife out of the sheath strapped to her calf. Jeremy's eyes got big.

"Don't go away, I'll be right back!"

Carol went into the living room while Jeremy made a lot of noise thrashing around on the bed and moaning. A minute later the Head Witchette peeked around the doorway with a big smile on her face.

"Look what I found!"

A lamp cord with the plug still on one end dangled from her hand. Carol came back into the room using the knife to strip away insulation from the other end. It was time to put on the rubber gloves.

"Let's see if we can jump-start whatever that little thing is between your legs. 'Kay?"

She plugged the cord into the wall outlet by the bed and held the end with the bare wires close to the target area. Jeremy was frozen still with fear, his threatened genitalia seemed to be retracting. Carol made a little feint jab and Jeremy shrieked behind the tape.

"Got something to tell me, hot-shot? Something about some of my property?"

Another little jab that came short. Jeremy jumped and started nodding his head frantically.

The tape came off with a sickening sound. The bare wires accidentally grazed Jeremy's protruding stomach, and the little man jumped and shrieked again, this time without the tape.

Carol looked concerned.

"Oopsie! That was a freebie I guess. Want some more?"

She dangled the wire down low again. Jeremy was close to tears.

"Sara. I told Sara about them, about the Chacmools. She's the only one I told, I swear!" Carol had to think about this. Sara was the most resourceful of the Witchettes, and also the best at lucid dreaming. This was looking real bad.

"Why did you tell her, you little shit?" Carol was livid. "Why her, of all people?"

Jeremy smiled shyly.

"I thought if I told her she might be, you know, grateful. And want to show me how much she was grateful."

Carol went red in the face. Her hands were shaking with rage.

"You sold me out so you could get laid?"

The former owner of two Chacmools let out a yell and jammed the electrical cord between Jeremy's legs as hard as she could. Jeremy screamed as his body jerked up once before a fuse blew and everything went dark.

Carol found the flashlight and checked to make sure she hadn't killed the little vermin bastard. He'd fainted and wet the bed. A wisp of smoke was coming from between his legs, but otherwise he was fine.

She left him tied up and put the tape back on his mouth. Needed to make a mental note to come back and untie him in a couple days.

Chapter 24

Sara

When Charlie Spider died, Sara took it the hardest. She'd been with Charlie for several years and had grown to depend on him to tell her what to do. She'd never been anything special before hooking up with Charlie and felt lost without him. Just another average-looking girl trying to figure out what to do with herself. She had calm brown eyes and mousy brown hair that never looked quite right. In spite of having a decent figure, the quiet young woman was otherwise so plain no one ever noticed her.

Charlie's sometimes-strange sexual needs took priority, but everyone at the mansion was trained in more practical things as well. Some of the women practiced various martial arts or studied acting or homeopathy. Others, like Carol, took managerial classes.

Sara studied karate. Charlie also sent her to the East coast several times for training in the art of tracking and stalking, and she was good. It was nothing for her to go into

Carol's room and find the hiding spot for the Chacmools. There was a pattern to the faint dust on the floor that clearly showed Carol's normal movements. Sara could see the difference in the way the dust was moved near the wall. The loose panel above the window was a little high for her, she wasn't as tall as Carol, but she managed to pull the box with the idols out with no problem.

* * *

With Charlie gone, Sara had spent days wandering around the mansion and the grounds, looking for something, but she didn't know what. She watched a lot of television, something she hadn't done in years. The other women had always acted as if she was a little off, and Sara becoming even more introverted than usual didn't seem to be helping.

She latched onto the Food Channel and soon immersed herself in cooking. She cooked huge meals for the other women and was always experimenting with something new. Before long she had gained another skill and ten pounds. Then the dreams began.

Charlie came to her in ordinary dreams, then in frighteningly real lucid dreams. The image of Charlie was clear, but she could never make out what he was saying.

She lost her appetite for food, but not for cooking. Before long Sara had lost the extra weight, but the dreams were causing her to slip into a deep depression. She was adrift.

The little lecherous guy who was supposed to be Charlie's nephew ate some of her leftover quiche once and, after that, started hanging around the mansion whenever Carol was gone.

"Hey Sara, I heard somebody saying you have dreams about my dear dead uncle. He tell you any secrets in those dreams?"

"No. He talks to me, but I can't understand what he's saying. You know, Carol said she doesn't want you hanging around here. Maybe you should leave."

"Carol can go take a flying leap. Hey, I know a little secret. It's about dreaming and my uncle in fact. Maybe we can work something out here."

Charlie's nephew told her about some gold statues that were supposed to be magic. Sara thought this might be what she'd been looking for after Charlie died and asked the little man to tell her more, but he wanted her to do all kinds of sex things with him first. She finally relented. It was pretty awful.

When she found out about the little statues, she simply went into Carol's room, studied the floor closely, and found the hidden box.

The diary in the box told the full story. She learned that if the two Chacmools were put by a person's ears and the third, missing idol was placed on the eyes while that person was in lucid dreaming, the dreams would manifest themselves — they would become real. The diary told of the history of the Chacmools, revealing that the third one was probably lost hundreds of years ago when a Spanish treasure ship went down off the Florida Keys. That would explain Carol's recent trip to Florida, but she had obviously come back without it.

Everything went in the box and Sara carefully put it back in Carol's room. She spent the next few days shadowing Carol whenever she was around. One day she heard the head Witchette talking on the phone and caught some names. Later she found a receipt from a private investigation agency in Carol's papers and put it all together. There was an investigator on the case called Saul Thorpe who was looking for a man in Florida who might have the missing Chacmool. Jeremy said he had been in Key West with Carol, so she'd start there.

After scraping together as much money as she could, Sara grabbed the idols and diary and headed for Florida. All she had to do was find this man Saul, follow him until he had something, then take it.

Once she had the third Chacmool, there was no reason to screw around. Sara was going to bring Charlie back.

Chapter 25

It's Better in the Keys

Another long road to nothing. Saul had gone from Chok across the state and south to Flamingo. What a waste. Flamingo was even smaller, and he got zip for info. Wasted several hours on that. Only saw one bike going there too. Big dresser Harley with a fucking windshield. Saul took a shot anyway, hit the windshield with a big noise. Didn't go down.

Left Flamingo pissed. Two bicycles coming the other way. Got the lead bike, but he was only doing about forty because of the winding road. Didn't even see if the bicycle went down. Waste of gum, those bicycles. Better to just bump 'em with a fender.

* * *

Later that afternoon, Saul's mood improved when he got into the Keys. Figured he'd go on down to Key West, check on the rental boat, take it from there.

Bridges, lots of bridges. Saul had never gummed a bike on a bridge before. The thought made him smile.

Stopped for a beer and a sandwich and looked at the map. There was a bridge up next that was seven miles long. Saul liked the odds. He'd seen a few bikes in traffic already. Maybe after this job, make a couple extra passes over that sucker.

He waited until the traffic thinned before going up on the long bridge. Saul was pumped.

"Come on, come on! Give me something here! This is too good! A little Jap bike, a moped for fuck's sake! Anything!"

He was chewing a big wad and his eyes strained, looking up ahead. Then he was over halfway across the bridge.

"I promise not to shoot any stray dogs for a week! Okay, how about I lay off my mom for the money she owes me? Come on here! Give me something!" Saul pounded his fist on the steering wheel. "Okay. I promise not to pick my nose in restaurants anymore!"

Up ahead in the distance, Saul could see a small black shape coming out of the bright glare of the bridge. "Please, please, oh please, let it be!"

It was.

"YES!" Saul hopped up and down in his seat. "Yes, oh thank you! Yes!"

Quick check behind. Clear. No one else in front. Perfect.

Big, fat, dirty biker on a chopped Harley with no helmet.

Spit the wad in hand. Lob.

It was like hitting the sweet spot on a golf ball. Saul knew it was perfect as soon as it left his hand.

The impact flattened the gum to the size of a CD on the biker's forehead. Saul watched the rear-view mirror with his whole being as the hands came off the handlebars and grabbed at the head. The bike veered off to the side and glanced off the guardrail. The big blob of biker came off the motorcycle and bounced once off the top of the guardrail before disappearing over the side of the bridge.

Saul immediately broke into maniacal laughter. He looked down from the mirror just as the van touched the rail, throwing a shower of sparks and putting a crease in the side. He didn't care. He had never been more alive.

* * *

The first motel in Key West had a sign boasting how many rooms it had. Should have a vacancy, didn't look expensive. Get a room, check around a little on the boat thing, find some action.

Chapter 26

The First Motel in Key West

André, the assistant manager of the Big Pelican Happy Nice Motel, had seen it all in his relatively short career in hotel/motel management. Cheapskates, drunks, cheaters, dopers, criminals, runaways, perverts, hookers, people hiding from someone, people looking for someone, rich people slumming, bums trying to move up, and every combination thereof.

He glanced up from his computer screen and regarded the big, shaved-head, bulldog-looking piece of work in the tight black t-shirt and jeans with the sunglasses stuck on top of his shiny head. Another tough-guy loser asshole.

"Good afternoon, sir, may I help you?"

"I need a room with a big bed and a big TV."

"Yes, sir. Let me see what we have available." André looked at his computer screen and tapped a few keys.

"You got fuck movies on the TV here?"

"Um, we have basic cable in all our rooms, sir. There's a special on giant pandas tonight on Discovery, I believe,"

André said without looking up from the screen, "and the Food Channel has another of those fascinating shows on eel recipes later on."

Saul grunted and frowned. André smiled.

"Room 325C, the Presidential Suite should be to your liking, sir. We just had the carpet cleaned this morning."

Saul narrowed his eyes at the man behind the counter and slapped down a credit card. André swiped the card, showed where to sign, and handed over the key, smiling.

"Enjoy your stay in Key West, sir!" he said to the back of the shaved head as it walked out the door. André knew that room was the furthest back in the motel, but he didn't know if the latest carpet cleaning had gotten the vomit smell out or not.

Chapter 27

Taco Bob returns to Panama City

"Smoke 'em if you got 'em!"

A crisp, clear morning in St. Augustine found Pete and me still smiling about our big day fishing. We gave the high points of the previous day a good going over while we laid waste to platters of eggs, sausage, hashbrowns, and toast at a place just down from the marina. Nothing like offshore fishing to put the appetite on a body.

"I shore got to catch me another of those wahoo someday, Taco. That was some kind of run that fish put on me when he hit." He pointed with his fork, "You going to eat that sausage?"

I gave him a look of warning.

"As a matter of fact, I am. I'm saving it for dessert. But yeah, we definitely need to do this again. It don't get much better, you know."

Pete was giving hard looks to some pies up on a counter.

"I'm with you on that, Taco, about as close as it gets to a perfect day. Them pies are calling me." He gave the waitress a wave and got his order in. I went with just a refill on the coffee to keep from hurting myself.

"Only strange thing all day was that other boat kept going by. That many miles of water there ought to be enough spots you don't have to be following a charter boat all day."

While Pete ate pie, we agreed some people just weren't raised considerate.

We settled the bill and walked out looking at bluebird skies and chewing on toothpicks. After a good round of handshakes, Pete headed back toward North Carolina while I worked my way west toward the panhandle section of the state.

When I had first come to Florida from Texas, I'd stayed over by Panama City for a while at this little RV park. That was where I'd caught my first Florida trout, so I figured I might give that area another look.

* * *

The RV park I'd stayed at before was right where I'd left it. There were a few different travel trailers, but other than that it looked about the same. Only a block from the beach, the park had a tropical feel to it with all the cabbage palms, gulls squawking overhead, and the smell of salt in the breeze.

I found the lady running the place, and she was happy to see me and wanted to know what I'd been up to. Told her I planned to catch some trout and write a bestseller when I got back to Key West. This must have been good news or reminded her of something because she smiled big and laughed a little on her way outside. I followed her out of the office, and she gave my truck and boat a good looking over.

"You got yourself a nice boat these days, and it looks like you're eating regular. Something to be said for that."

A shiny blue Ferrari was just pulling out of the park onto the highway. I gave her a questioning look and she gave me back a shrug.

"Never seen it before. Your old spot over behind the washroom is open if you want it. Heard yesterday people were catching some nice fish out on the pier. Good luck." She headed back in to answer the phone, giggling and saying something to herself about bestsellers.

Before I even got set up at the campsite, a few of the folks who had been there before showed up. Turns out I'd been the talk of the park since leaving. Some new folks came by wanting to meet the fella who'd built the smoker and had the big party.

Come dark, we went on over and made up a little fire, then stood around and told stories and had a drink or two. I told the park folks about my plans to travel around the state and catch trout, and said I'd come to see if there were any left swimming around there we could invite for dinner.

*

First thing the next morning, I was knee-deep fishing at my favorite spot along the beach. Other than a few early walkers and circling sea birds, it was just me and the fish. I caught a couple nice trout on plastic grub-tail jigs before something cut my line. I had my big ice chest with me, so I decided to take care of them that would cut my line and relieve me of my fishing lure. I put on a small silver spoon and a little bit of wire leader and soon enough started dropping mackerel in on the ice.

With my ice chest on a little handcart I'd borrowed from the folks at the park, I packed up and went to check on the pier. There were several small trout and another nice one waiting for me, and the macs were thick. By early afternoon I had plenty of fish, so I wished luck to the few fisherman on the pier and pulled my cooler back to the park.

The little smoker I'd built out of scrap wood and tin was still there, all right, so I got her fired up. The smell from the fish in the smoker was the signal for everyone to break out some food for a big community dinner. We ate and drank and stood around the fire telling stories after dark till way late.

By the time I finally got to bed, I was feeling good. I realized that without any pressing financial concerns, woman problems, or escaped convicts looking to shoot, strangle, stab, or blow me up, life could be mighty sweet. It was a feeling I hoped to get to know well.

* * *

Smoked Trout

Trout fillets with the skin still on (Mackerel work real good too for this. Actually, mackerel work better, but trout are pretty good too.)
Herb and garlic marinade (Store-bought is fine. Italian dressing also works.)
Cajun or creole seasoning
Hickory, pecan, or mesquite wood chips soaked in water

Put fish fillets in a plastic bag and add marinade. You don't need a whole lot, about 6–8 ounces per gallon bag of fillets. Set this in the fridge while you get the smoker going.

As soon as the fire burns down to coals, place the fillets skin side down on the wire racks. Before you close up the smoker, sprinkle the fish with seasoning and throw some damp wood chips on the coals. It usually takes about an hour or two for the fish to cook. Add a few more wood chips as needed. Fish should be golden brown and flake easily when done.

If you have any left over, just crumble the fish up in a bowl with some spices, pickle relish, and mayonnaise. Makes some kinda good spread for crackers.

Chapter 28

Saul in KW

It was the smallest motel room Saul had ever seen. There was a big bed, a good-sized television, and nothing else in the room. Just enough space to walk to the tiny bathroom. Saul turned on the noisy air conditioner that took up the lower half of the only window and lay out on the bed just for a minute to rest his eyes.

When he woke it was dark. He turned on the lamp bolted to the wall above the bed. The room didn't smell very good. Get a quick shower before checking out the town.

Took a look at the local titty bar. He'd seen better. This one had cheap drinks at least. Got him ready for some action.

Checked a couple of bars. No shortage of bars in this town. Started looking for the right woman. Should be sitting alone. Get close, maybe talk to her a little, hope she goes to the can. Slip a roofie in her drink, ten minutes later she'd be smashed. Bouncer in Atlanta even helped him put this cute little blonde in the van once.

"Too much to drink. Got some bad news about her mother today, cancer. I better get her home."

Had a lot of fun with that one, thought about keeping her a while. Didn't do it though; that would be sick.

Saul didn't get any roofie action on Duval Street, but he got pretty drunk.

Next day he checked the docks. Asked around the marina to see if any of the rocket scientists around there knew anything. Rental boat thing was a bust, but this one stoner cleaning up a charter boat said there was a guy had been looking for work. Guy stopped coming around, then showed up in a nice flats boat one day. Boat description was right. Stoner gave Saul the eye and asked what he wanted him for. Saul showed the burnout his PI badge. Said the man's brother needed a kidney transplant. Real important he find the guy.

Stoner got helpful. Said once he saw the guy's boat on a trailer parked in a yard over on Mango Street, the house with the brown trim next to the two-story on the corner. Saul thanked him, said he might have just saved a life.

* * *

Over on Mango, it didn't look like anyone was there.

"They're not there."

Neighbor. Dumpy old bag walking up behind him in a housedress, long cigarette in her hand. Probably kept an eye on the street from inside while looking at soap operas. Saul stepped back from the front door and smiled.

"Morning, ma'am. Would you happen to know when they'll be back?"

The old bat gave him a look.

"Who wants to know?"

Saul was ready.

"Florida Lottery Prize Patrol ma'am. Looking for a man that keeps his boat here. Real important I talk to him."

Saul flashed his badge.

"They left this morning to go visit her brother in North Carolina. You must be looking for Taco Bob. He parks his truck and boat here sometimes, but he left a few days ago."

A name.

"Yes ma'am. As a matter of fact, Taco Bob is the person I need to talk to. I've been authorized by the lottery commission to compensate anyone who can help me locate one of our win... I mean, one of the people we need to interview."

Saul pulled out a stack of bright, flashy, multi-colored, buck-apiece, scratch-off tickets and let them unfold almost to the ground.

"My word! I don't know where he went, Orlando maybe. Has some girlfriend there. I'm taking care of their cats while they're gone." The woman never took her eyes off the string of lottery cards. "Let me just look inside and see if there isn't a number or something by the phone."

* * *

For fifteen dollars worth of tickets, Saul had the phone number and address of the girlfriend in Orlando.

Chapter 29
Bandit

Three helicopters circled a huge traffic jam on Interstate 10. A truck matching the description of the now-famous Southernmost Bandit's had been spotted westbound by a police helicopter. The other two choppers were news media getting footage for the evening news of the massive jam caused by the twenty-five police cars that had the wrong truck surrounded in the middle of the road.

Drivers rubber-necking in the eastbound lanes had plowed into each other and traffic was stopped for several miles in that direction, too.

* * *

With a big breakfast under his belt, a cooler full of sandwiches, and a remarkable evening with a surprisingly limber and athletic young woman to think about, Julian continued on his journey.

He got fuel in Valdosta and checked the truck. Of the eighteen wheels on the whole rig, a couple tires on the trailer didn't look very good. One had thrown the cap already, and another was about to go.

Julian decided to go back into Florida and head west on I-10 to make some time. He still hadn't seen the news and hoped not too many people were looking for him.

Coming up on the interstate just before Chipley, he could see traffic was backed up bad. Looked like it was going to be SR 90 instead. He passed under the interstate bridge and turned around in the parking lot of a boarded-up, old motel. One of the rear tires on the tractor caught a sharp piece of metal that cut deep. The metal came out and hit the inside of the fender with a bang, but the tire held.

Julian pulled back on the road after a truck pulling a boat and a bright red Hummer went by. He headed north for the next westbound road. He was hearing the music softly now, thinking of Georgia, heading for home.

Chapter 30

Taco Bob and the Big Bend in the Road

"Nature coast trout!"

It took me a while to break camp and say goodbye to everyone there in the park the next day, but I finally got her done and hit the road.

Drove up to catch I-10 for the run east; but when I got up there I could see the traffic was down to a crawl, so I turned around and backtracked a bit to find another route. I could have swore I seen the same truck that almost ran me over down by Daytona. Must be a lot of that kind of truck.

There's a lot of prime trout habitat all along the western edge of the state they call the Big Bend. It's mostly miles of oyster bars and sawgrass swamp that has to pass for land, and countless freshwater creeks mixing with the Gulf. Not much in the way of big towns along the coast till you get down toward Tampa. Place I'd read about and had in mind to try out was called Cedar Key.

Cedar Key is another real old town like Key West — old for Florida at least. Like Key West, a railroad going in there was what first put it on the map. Back in the 1800s, about the only ports between Cuba and New Orleans were Key West, Tampa, and Cedar Key. Seriously bucking the statewide trend, the town of Cedar Key still has about the same number of people it had almost two hundred years ago.

There's a few little scrub oak and sawgrass islands out just beyond Cedar Key. Not much of anybody living there these days except 'coons, birds, and snakes. And I had no intention of so much as setting foot on any of those islands, much less spending any time exploring them. Just fish the shallow grass flats around the islands and find a nice trout or two for recipe-testing purposes. Maybe relax in the evenings with a crossword puzzle and watch some color TV, then sleep on a big, comfortable motel bed.

I had Cedar Key all figured out by the time I hit the first bridge.

Chapter 31

Sara

The humidity was the first surprise for Sara in Key West. Still wearing her drab Spider Cult clothes, she started sweating as soon as she stepped out of the airport terminal. In the cab on her way to Old Town, Sara had time to once again think about her tenuous situation. She not only had no idea how to find the man called Saul Thorpe, she didn't even know for sure he was in Key West.

A quick look at the people wandering around Duval Street and a stop in a shop or two, and Sara was wearing the kind of comfortable clothes she needed to keep cool and fit in. Not that she really needed the tourist clothes, no one noticed her anyway.

When she was a young girl in school, Sara used to rebel against her boring too-normal appearance and went out of her way to stand out and be noticed. Years later, when Charlie Spider sent her to tracker school, they taught her how to use her uncommonly common physical presence to her advantage. She learned to blend in so well that after a while her teachers didn't even remember if she'd attended classes.

One of the things Charlie had written about in his books was inner silence. He said that if people could learn to silence the constant thoughts we all have, their senses would become more attuned to the world, both inner and outer. He also said that though it sounded like an easy thing to do, in reality it was damn hard. Sara agreed with Charlie. It was hard, but not impossible.

After years of struggle, Sara learned to quiet her mind for short periods of time. She became more aware of the myriad things going on all around at every moment that affect people's lives. The intervals of inner silence also seemed to make her more adept at lucid dreaming.

But she never told Charlie. Even though he was the one who opened the door for her, Sara could tell he had never experienced the depth of silence that she had. Charlie had been a master bullshit artist with charisma to spare, but he was never a seer.

* * *

Sara expected Key West to be a day at the beach, but it seemed more like a day at the races. The Conch Republic turned out to be a busy place. She carefully navigated the streets filled with out-of-state cars that left a faint odor of suntan lotion and exhaust in their wake. Bicycles and noisy little motorcycles were competing for road space with Conch Tour trains and delivery trucks. Everyone wore shorts, and a lot of people seemed to be either coming from a bar, going to a bar, or both.

The former Witchette took in the sights, sounds and smells of this warm, humid place that had a different underlying energy than LA. People here were always going somewhere too, but there wasn't nearly the urgency. She got the impression that a lot of people felt that just being in Key West was enough of an accomplishment to hold them for a while.

A few tourists were milling around a spot near the water where some yellow crime scene tape hung from a couple of leaning palm trees. One of those big bulldozer machines with the scoop on front was there, and people were taking turns standing in front of it for pictures. But something was different here, so Sara quietly stood next to a section of broken down fence to see if she could find out what this place was. Two women in big hats and brightly colored clothing came walking up with their husbands close behind.

"This is it, Agnes! The place on the news where that marker thing was stolen!"

The other woman picked up on it.

"Frank, come take my picture here! The neighbors are gonna shit! Look, there's the crime scene tape still! Oh my God, this is just like America's Most Wanted!"

After they left, Sara wanted to get closer to the spot in front of the big machine, but she had to wait when a well-dressed young woman and a camera crew walked up. The crew spent a few minutes getting ready, then the woman held a microphone and spoke.

"Is the hair right? This breeze is fucking with my hair! Joey, if my hair isn't right ..."

The woman reporter pointed at the cameraman and narrowed her eyes until another man holding a big card with writing on it assured her the hair was fine. The woman gave the hair a couple of pats anyway and stuck her chest out a little before speaking.

"That's right, Peter. Even though the famous monument marking the Southernmost Point in the Continental US was stolen by the Southernmost Bandit in a blatant disregard for all that is right and decent here in the Crotch Republic, people are still flocking to this spot. In fact, the area where the monument once stood is more popular than ever. All right, what are you bozos laughing about this time?"

* * *

The news crew finally left, and Sara walked closer to where the monument had been. There was definitely something here. She sat on the sand a few feet from the big earth-moving machine. As soon as she sat down she went into a dream, but she was still somewhat aware of what was going on around her. She was experiencing dual perceptions for the first time.

At the same time a fat man with painfully red knees was taking pictures, in the dream there was only the water and land and no people in sight. Sara could tell the place where she sat was a power spot used by many. There were no signs of man, other than bare footprints in the sand and marks along the water's edge where canoes had come.

A young couple laughing, holding cans of beer, walked around Sara sitting on the ground. The dream took her to a ceremony on the power spot. Dark people with dark faces chanting in the moonlight. Someone lay on the sandy beach and the others slowly moved around in some sort of dance. Sara could feel the power coming from the earth.

There was a huge cruise ship off in the distance and a little boy ran by squealing with his mother close behind. In the dream, Sara was lying on the sand. She could feel energy flowing from the earth into her body, and then back into the earth. An exchange of power. The dark forms chanted louder, deafening. There was a flash of gold at each ear; she thought she heard Charlie's voice calling to her. The ground began to tremble. The sky was flashing gold. The gold light came closer to her eyes and she could almost see Charlie's face. There was a voice, a loud voice.

"Hey! How about somebody tell her to move!"

There was a tourist woman kneeling in front of Sara, shaking her arm.

"You better get out of the way, miss."

The dream was gone, but the earth still rumbled and trembled. Sara looked behind her and saw a man on the big yellow machine, waving at her to move.

"Come on, Honey! Park it somewhere else will ya? I got a job to do here!"

Sara stood by the fence again and the big machine roared away to a waiting flatbed truck.

* * *

The breeze was pushing her. Sara walked slowly away from the place where the monument had been. It had to be a power place, something Charlie had spoken of often, but she had never experienced before. It left her with a feeling of accomplishment, and a strange energy.

She went with the gentle wind and let it carry her thoughts away. Walking effortlessly, she began to feel the warmth and texture of the ground through the soles of her shoes. The breeze carried smells and sounds from the sea as well as the land, and the sky became even clearer and lost its glare. There was a black boy dressed like the Hip-Hop boys she saw in LA. He was sitting behind a table covered with the skeletons of sea beings. He was looking at her.

"Hey, pretty lady! You want to buy some of these nice shells today? Look at the colors here. You ever see that shade of pink before? Don't have these back home I bet!"

Sara smiled at the boy and walked by. She stopped and closed her eyes. She could feel the earth with all her senses. The earth touched her inside and out and she felt a small ripple down her spine. Turning slowly she opened her eyes and was looking down a walkway, a short narrow wooden pier. There was an old black man with a big straw hat sitting at the end of the pier. She could see the whites of his eyes as he stared right at her.

Chapter 32
Taco Bob in Cedar Key

"I still don't know if I was dreaming."

There ain't a whole hell of a lot to Cedar Key. A few mom-and-pop restaurants and motels, some bait shops and a scattering of weathered houses. I got a motel room with a kitchenette so I could try out some fancy trout recipes if I had any luck out on the water.

The next morning I threw the boat in the water early and went to check on the fish. It was cool when I put in, and it looked like it wanted to be cloudy. I ran up close to one of the islands and started throwing a cast net. Pretty soon I had a few dozen sardines and pinfish for bait. I eased around and located a big area of shallow water with a good sea grass bottom. Looked like trout habitat to me.

I set a pinfish on a float out the back and drifted over the area. Put a sardine on a float and was casting that one from the front of the boat. Those sardines didn't ever last too long before something was wanting to eat their little asses. Ladyfish are usually a foot and a half to two foot long and silver; a pretty fish that does a lot of jumping out of the water. Tied into several of those.

There were little black sea bass, slimy ol' catfish, puffers, redfish, mackerel, and plenty of trout. The trout ran mostly small, but I finally got into some nice ones that were going around three pounds. They did their usual show with coming to the surface and thrashing around, then trying to break the line when they got close in.

Just as I slipped one of those nice dinner-size trout into the icebox, the pole in back went over double. I jumped back, pulled it out of the rod-holder and about a hundred pounds of tarpon came completely out of the water about thirty feet from the boat.

It seems like even when you're expecting it, a tarpon on your line is always a surprise. I wasn't expecting it, and I was mighty surprised. I did my best to hold on while that fish made a hard run away from the boat. About a hundred yards out he made another jump and the line gave out. I was mighty disappointed, but glad I'd had the chance to air one out at least.

With dinner in the cooler, I went exploring around the islands the rest of the day. There were a few other boats, but mostly they were bigger boats headed way offshore. Must be an airport in the area, since there was a lot of small plane traffic.

By late afternoon, I had explored myself up north along the coastline a few miles and decided to start heading back in. When I looked back toward Cedar Key, all I could see was gray. There was a fog bank slowly coming across the water, and it was thick. I ran up to the fog then slowed to a crawl since I couldn't see a thing. I wasn't really worried until I turned on the GPS and found out the batteries were dead. The boat compass got me going in the right general direction at least.

That whole area was full of shallows and channels and oyster bars. I spent a couple hours working my way along and found a couple of oyster bars the hard way. It was getting late in the day and the fog hadn't lifted a bit.

I came up on an island just as it got dark, and decided to give the place a look. I got the boat tied off and anchored, then got my flashlight out and looked around a little at the beach area. It was still so foggy I couldn't see much of anything. I got some skeeter dope on my arms and face and went looking for some firewood.

I always carry a little frying pan and some cooking stuff on my boat since I found myself in a similar situation once before. I cleaned and cooked the trout and swatted skeeters while thinking about my already-paid-for motel room back in Cedar Key.

Damn fog never let up a bit, so I got out my poncho, found a soft spot in the sand, and tried to get some sleep. I kept thinking at least I didn't have to worry about anybody sneaking up on me. Which made me realize I'd had an uneasy feeling for days, like I was being followed.

* * *

Sometime during the night I got up to check on the boat and found a young boy sitting there in the dark. This was a bit odd, since I hadn't heard any noises on the island that sounded like people lived out there. It was also odd because he reminded me of a little Indian kid I'd seen once in Chokoloskee.

When I asked him if he lived out there, the boy just smiled and jumped in my boat and motioned for me to come, pointing at the compass on the console of my boat. I put the flashlight on the compass and he pointed with the tip of his smallest finger at south-southwest. His eyes shone black in the foggy moonlight. When I asked him if that was the way to Cedar Key, he nodded and jumped out of the boat. He gave me a big shy smile and then ran down the beach into the fog. I went over to my spot on the beach and finally got back to sleep.

At first light, the fog was still thick, but I was ready to do something even if it was wrong. Between the nightbirds, bugs, raccoons, and little Indian kids, I hadn't had one of my better night's sleep. Thinking about my visitor, I checked my fingers and got the right amount. I wished I'd had the presence of mind to check my fingers when I'd seen the kid.

I got under way and eased the boat slowly into the fog, holding a dead-on south-southwest course. There was a big shark tooth lying next to the compass. I figured either a really big shark had had some dental work done in my boat during the night, or else my little visitor left me a present. The tooth put me in mind of my time in the Everglades and made me think again about checking on Mr. Small.

The fog never did burn off, but I did finally come up on a channel marker by mid-morning. I got out my chart and checked the number. Sure enough, I was right on the money for Cedar Key.

I didn't get out of the fog that day until I drove over the last bridge headed back onto the mainland.

* * *

Fried Trout

Two small skinned trout fillets, or one big
one cut in half
Breading mix (I like hushpuppy mix and
Italian bread crumbs together)
Vegetable oil
Salt and pepper to taste

Put your breading mix in a plastic or paper bag. (I carry a gallon ziplock bag with the mix already in it on my boat.)

Place damp fillets in the bag and give 'em a good shaking till they're well coated with breading.

Get your driftwood fire going strong and rocks or shells or even an anchor next to it to hold the frying pan. Get the oil hot before putting the fish in the pan.

Fish should turn golden brown in just a few minutes. When fish flakes with a pocketknife, it's ready. Great by itself, or with a can of beans.

Chapter 33

Southernmost

The tarp blew off the monument sometime during the night. Julian didn't notice until he was making a fuel and coffee stop outside of Houston around daybreak. It'd been a long day and night of driving, and he was too tired to do anything about it. He hadn't had any sleep since the few hours he'd spent in the arms of the young woman in Georgia.

The story of the monument theft was on the small television behind the cashier, but Julian was too worn out to care he'd made the national news. By the time he'd paid for his gas and coffee, a small crowd had formed around the truck. As Julian approached, the buzzing, picture-taking crowd pulled their eyes away from the now-famous brightly colored monument on the flat-bed trailer. They gawked at the disheveled-looking young man carrying a large styrofoam cup of coffee with the Texas state flag imprinted on the side. An old man stepped from the crowd as Julian started to get back in the truck.

"You're him, aren't ya sonny? You're the one we been hearing about on the TV!" You could have heard a pin drop at the fueling complex. "Can you tell us, Mr. Southernmost Bandit, just what it is you aim to do with this thing?"

Julian was a little taken aback by the crowd, but was too tired to give it much thought. The music went up from a whisper to a hum in his road-weary mind. He rallied his strength.

"I'm bringing this monument to its rightful place to mark the true Southernmost Point in the Continental US. The people of the great state of Texas have been denied for too long the honor that is rightfully theirs. I will bring this great gift to the southernmost tip of Texas, or I will die trying!"

The music from an old Clint Eastwood western was roaring in his ears now. He took a sip of coffee, which showed the Texas flag on the cup to the camcorder that was taking the footage that would be sold to the highest bidder of the television networks later that morning.

A small boy wearing a t-shirt that said, "I Love Texas" on the back, ran and hugged Julian's knees as a groggy but defiant Julian looked over at a woman from Arizona who was taking the photograph that would become famous in a few hours.

* * *

The Governor of Florida watched in horror as the first of the news helicopters showed the live feed of his monument on the back of a truck heading toward the southern tip of Texas. The Governor had called Washington and demanded something be done to stop the truck before it reached its destination.

* * *

The gubernatorial elections were coming up in Texas as well, so the current and hoping-to-be-soon-re-elected Governor of the Yellow Rose State ordered the Texas Highway Patrol to escort the renegade truck until any directives came in from Washington.

* * *

In Washington, the President was busy with a delegation from China who were being a real pain in the ass about wanting to do an above-ground nuclear weapons test on a neighboring country.

* * *

State Police cars were in front and back of the truck, while a growing number of lawyers driving luxury cars and SUVs jockeyed for position behind the police escort. Several helicopters flew overhead, and there were people waving and taking pictures from alongside the road.

Julian was fighting to keep himself awake and the truck on the road. He was less than an hour from home when he started losing tires. The tire that had taken the piece of metal blew with a sickening squeal, and he lost control of the rig. He went off on the shoulder of the road for a hundred yards and popped two trailer tires before getting back up on the highway. The troopers riding escort were suddenly wide awake and a minivan full of photographers that had been run off the road had to make an emergency restroom stop.

The residents of Brownspot had heard the news and were gathering in the town square, wearing their best clothes and bearing gift baskets of food and flowers for the returning hero. A brass band rehearsed patriotic songs, and satellite news trucks from across the region frantically set up shop.

By the time he passed through neighboring Brownsville, only a few miles from home, Julian had hundreds of cars and trucks following him and dozens of helicopters and small airplanes buzzing overhead. The wheel bearings of the trailer were pouring black smoke, and several news organizations reporting live speculated wildly about what had caused the truck to momentarily lose control earlier.

As an exhausted Julian slowly drove the smoking, squealing truck the last few hundred yards into the town square of Brownspot, both sides of the road were filled with cheering, waving, excited people. Children threw flowers in the path of the truck, young maidens sang heartfelt love songs, and many along the route felt overcome with emotion at the sight of the brave young man with this noble gift to his people, his family, his town, and his state.

The heat from the burning wheel bearings had cooked the brakes, but Julian managed to stop the truck in the center of town, directly in front of the camera crews, with some help from the front half of the town barbershop.

Thousands cheered in the streets, balloons came from everywhere, the town band played “The Good, the Bad, and the Ugly” like never before, and millions more watching on TV across the country were caught up in the moment.

Julian opened the door of the truck and triumphantly raised his arms above his head before collapsing into the arms of several still-singing young maidens.

Chapter 34

The Governor of Florida

The Governor of Florida made little sobbing noises as he sat in front of the television with his head in his hands. An aide patted the distraught Governor on the back and handed him a pillow to hug.

"That's all right sir, you did everything you could." The aide knew it was a lame thing to say, but he was emotionally drained himself after four hours of watching the television coverage of the Southernmost Bandit.

Someone turned off the television showing a disoriented but smiling young man with lipstick prints covering his face and several microphones in front of him.

* * *

An emergency meeting of the Governor and his team followed. There was a hell of a lot of media attention out there on this thing, and so far it looked like Florida was full of nincompoops who couldn't stop some kid from single-handedly walking off with several tons of brightly colored concrete monument.

After several options were tossed around involving covert military action by the Florida National Guard to recover the monument, it was decided that the best plan was to focus attention on getting a new monument as soon as possible. Get the people of Florida involved. Have a telethon to raise money, maybe get schoolchildren to have a contest for the design of the new monument. Something.

The newest member of the Governor's re-election team came up with the grabber. The tall man with flecks of gray in his short dark hair stood before the Governor and his anxious aides.

"What we need is a party, but not just any party. We need to have the biggest benefit concert in the history of the state, and we need to have it right there on the Southernmost site in Key West!"

There were nods of agreement in the room. The aide continued.

"But first we have to get Key West cranking, wake the town up. Have them move their big blowout, Fantasy Fest, up to the same week as the concert. Then throw in the Hemingway Festival, Bike Week, maybe even a special four-day lobster season."

He had everyone's full attention now.

"Then for the Grand Finale — the benefit concert itself — we get Marty the Manatee to come out of retirement as the headliner."

Everyone was smiling. The Governor stood and stretched like a bear coming out of hibernation. He gave his newest aide a wink and a slap on the back.

"That's it people; let's make this work! Somebody get Key West on the phone. Get some committees organizing this thing while I fly out to see Marty and get him on board."

Chapter 35
Marty

Years ago, Marty Jingles had been just another musician kicking around Key West. Once, on a drunken dare, he wore gray clothes and colored his skin and hair the same color gray. Since he had the facial features and physique pretty close already, he was a natural as Marty the Manatee. He quickly became the hottest act in Key West. Then he wrote the song.

"Tequila Breakfast" became the anthem across the country for people dissatisfied with their jobs, climate, and/or life. The song made Marty a superstar, but he somehow managed to keep from flaming-out and kept writing songs, touring, and making money.

After a few years he retired to a small island called Punta Margarita, which he picked up cheap from a struggling banana republic, and started investing in the US stock market. Since all the good causes had been spoken for, Marty launched a "Save the Bikers" campaign that brought him even greater notoriety and helped his Harley Davidson stock soar.

He hadn't been to Key West recently because his popularity caused near riots anytime he was spotted in public. There were plenty of impersonators though. On any given day you could see a half-dozen singing manatees on the streets and in the bars of Key West. There was even talk of having an annual festival called Marty Gras and a Look-a-Like Contest similar to the one for Hemingway.

No doubt about it, a Marty the Manatee concert would be the biggest news since Key West seceded from the Union.

Chapter 36

Saul

Saul called in the name he had gotten from the neighbor in Key West. LA said they needed more than "Taco Bob," but it was a start.

Some news: Job was getting bigger. There was an additional person on the contract now, woman named Sara. Same fee plus expenses for finding her. Agency gave a description and faxed a picture.

Said the price was up on the little gold statue, too. Client wanted it bad all of a sudden. Extra fifteen thou to Saul for the location of the idol, thirty if it was in his hand. Told him there might be three idols out there. This kind of jack put the job in the head-busting category.

* * *

Got to Orlando just after dark. No bikes on the bridges coming up. Shame. Take the major highways, big job now.

Address for a small duplex apartment. One car in the driveway, no truck or boat. Some light from a streetlamp down the road. Knocked on the door.

"Evening ma'am. Looking for Mary Ann."

Young broad opened the inside door just enough to see out. Screen door still closed. She didn't look happy.

"She's not here. Does she know you?"

Saul gave her a quick flash of the badge.

"Actually, looking for Taco Bob. Federal Bureau of Unclaimed Checks, got something here for him." Held up an envelope.

"You can just leave it there by the door, and I'll give it to him if he passes by."

Looked like the woman wasn't going to open the screen door to take the envelope. Talking time's over, time to get serious.

Busted a fist through the screen to undo the latch. Woman didn't scream at least, just stepped back. Yanked open the screen door and started in. Something moving low. Suddenly there's a Doberman clamped down between the legs. A lot of pain there.

"Get 'em, Fluffy! Rip his nuts off!"

Woman was making some noise now.

Getting back away from the front door with the dog biting down hard. Went for the gun, but the dog saw it. Let go the jewels to chomp the hand. Fucker sure could bite. Woman ran out with a baseball bat and started in with that. She must have played a little ball at one time. Good swing.

Made it to the van when the dog went for a better grip. Got bit on the leg too. Woman was yelling and beating on the van with the bat. Time to get the fuck out of there.

"Come back soon, asshole! You can meet Fluffy's big brother!"

Probably not. Woman obviously has some sort of problem with visitors.

Chapter 37

Idols

The young woman walked out on the pier and sat right down on the rough wood planks in front of his chair before speaking.

"I wonder if you could help me. For some reason I think you can."

She reached inside her bag, took out a little gold figurine and handed it over. Mr. Willie looked at the strange figure in his hand, and then again at the young woman looking up at him with the calmest eyes he had ever seen. He glanced at his grandson standing on shore next to the seashell stand. Young Willie was staring out toward them. He must have seen something in the young woman as well.

"I'm looking for one of these."

She held up a second figurine, identical to the first.

"There's a third one in the set. It may have been on a Spanish treasure ship that went down somewhere around this part of the state."

Mr. Willie felt a strange compassion for the young woman. He wanted to help. His years of fishing alone for days at a time had made him intensely aware of the dangers of the sea. In his years living on land, he had become aware of the dangers of the land. The land was much more dangerous — it had more people. He could read people like he used to read the waves and the wind. This little woman was being totally open with him.

"You might want to be checking the Treasure Museum there in town, you know. Them folks got all kinds of stuff, gold and silver stuff. I imagine they got records show if something like this ever been brought in."

"My name is Sara. I am not the first to come here seeking the third Chacmool. There was a tall woman before me. If it was easy, she would have already found it and I wouldn't be here now. Has anyone else asked you about this, maybe a big man? A private detective named Saul Thorpe?"

He knew the answer, but thought about it a minute anyway.

"No, they ain't all that many people asking an old seashell seller about little gold statues lately," he gave Sara a wink. "That treasure stuff, it be mostly them folks running them museums with the big boats and big money these days."

Mr. Willie remembered what Taco Bob said about meeting up with the old man up in the mangrove swamps.

"You know, though, maybe I do know something here. Years ago, there be a man thought he going to find treasure that them old pirates buried somewhere along here. I thought the man be long dead by now, but I hear just a few days ago he still alive. All them other old timers along them Ten Thousand Islands got run off by them National Park people years ago. I sure don't know that man ever find him any treasure or not, but I know he was sure looking, them many years ago."

There was the smallest smile in the young woman's eyes.

"Well, it's a start."

Chapter 38
Carol

In one of her rare moments of weakness, Carol went back to the trailer park the next day to turn Jeremy loose. She went in armed with her knife and a big aerosol can of air freshener. For once, Jeremy seemed glad to see her. He started crying and thanking her as soon as she ripped the tape off his mouth.

"Save it, Jeremy. I should just let you rot here, but I'm afraid you might get loose somehow and start telling more people about my missing property, and I'm not to the point of actually murdering you. At least not yet."

Carol's anger made her momentarily forget the smell inside the trailer. Jeremy must have seen the rage in Carol's eyes and decided to be quiet for once.

"I want you where I can keep an eye on you." Carol pulled the diver's knife out of a bag and cut one of the ropes holding Jeremy's feet. "And I must admit, you did help out with the fortune teller when we were in Key West before."

Jeremy's beady little eyes lit up.

"Before? We're going back to Key West?"

The cretin had nearly maxed her gold card at a topless bar the last time. Fat chance of that happening again.

"Yes, my wormy little degenerate, we're going back. I had planned to patiently wait here for the PIs to find the third Chacmool and bring it to me. Then I could have, in my own time, taken control over anyone I wanted." Carol sighed and cut the other rope. "But since you ratted me out, I have to go find that skinny little bitch Sara and get my property back first."

Jeremy held his wrists up so Carol could unlock the handcuffs next. He started grinning at the mention of Sara.

"I wouldn't say skinny. She's actually kinda —"

Carol dropped the key and put the big knife between Jeremy legs. Jeremy froze. Carol spoke through clenched teeth.

"Be very careful here, my little slime slug. You don't want to get me upset again, do you?"

Jeremy shook his head in short little bursts. He had a very sincere look on his face.

"So that everyone here is on the same page, Jeremy," the knife slowly withdrew, "if you should ever come down with another case of the running stupids and tell anyone else about the Chacmools ..."

Carol threw the knife down at the mattress with all her strength. It went to the hilt between Jeremy's legs so close he was nicked on the leg. When Carol yanked back on the knife, a big tear opened up and mattress stuffing came out.

"We leave for the airport in an hour."

Chapter 39

Paradise Revisited

Carol and Jeremy got into Key West International about an hour after the Governor had called another press conference. This time it was held in Key West with the Mayor and City Council, where they went over the program of events planned for the next few days, culminating in the benefit concert for the new monument. Governor Walker proudly announced that he had just returned from a personal meeting with Marty the Manatee, and that Marty would be headlining the concert.

Luckily Carol had reservations at the Hilton, because within minutes of the press conference every room in Key West was booked. Carol had neglected to make reservations for Jeremy, however, so while the head Witchette took a relaxing bath, Jeremy frantically searched Key West for a place to stay.

It came down to either the last room at the Big Pelican Happy Lucky Motel, a ten-foot section of concrete drainage pipe next to the Naval Base, or a cardboard shipping box underneath the Stock Island Bridge. Though the bridge had the better view and the drainage pipe smelled the best, Jeremy went with the Big Pelican because they had cable.

* * *

The plan was to scope out the island, find Sara, and get the Chacmools back. Carol had contacted the PIs before she left LA and had them looking for Sara and the other two idols as well.

Maybe the agency's man would come through. She could pick up all three Chacmools in Florida before returning to California and gaining total control over any living thing on the planet. That was the plan anyhow.

By the next morning, however, when Carol finally got a cab and went to pick up Jeremy, the off-season sleepiness of Key West was already shattered.

Everywhere, people were rushing around getting ready for the first parade of Fantasy Fest coming up that night. The traffic was already bumper to bumper nearly to Key Largo. Bikers, college students, fishermen with boats, tourists in rental cars and RVs, National Guard troops in military vehicles, assorted freaks and oddballs in vans and old buses, and hundreds of delivery trucks crowded the Overseas Highway.

Every business in Key West had put in a rush order for extra everything for the big week. There were two large trucks filled with nothing but body paint and beads for Fantasy Fest. Since these two items made up the entire costume for a number of Fantasy Fest participants, the two trucks were given police escorts through the snarled traffic.

As Carol and Jeremy walked through Old Town, the Duval Street traffic went from its usual busy to completely jammed. Since the streets were filled with gridlocked traffic, the early bikers just thundered down the sidewalks clipping the occasional dog, cat, or tourist.

By 10 am, every bar in town was standing room only. The first of the beer riots started outside Sloppy Joe's when word spread about a shortage of Corona. Soon afterwards, a t-shirt shop was looted to the bare walls and burned when they ran out of Marty the Manatee extra large t-shirts.

The National Guard finally got in town and started helping the local police haul drunks and rioters to the high school, which had been set up as an emergency jail.

In the water surrounding Key West, hundreds of boats full of divers circled in the hot sun, waiting for the afternoon opening of the special four-day lobster season. Hundreds more boats were on their way, streaming down both coasts of the state. Mostly larger cabin cruisers and sail boats, but a few rag-tag old houseboats as well. Huge cruise ships scheduled to stop in Key West were suddenly booked to capacity. Several of the giant ships were steaming toward Key West, hoping for a shot at one of the few good anchorages left.

* * *

Carol and Jeremy managed to get to the edge of Old Town in one piece. Jeremy kept begging to go back and visit the Pink Snapper Lounge for old times sake, but Carol wasn't taking any chances on losing her assistant and having to go look for him. She opened her bag and pulled out the special dog collar she'd bought in LA before they left. It was part of the deal for Jeremy to come along, but he still whined when he saw it.

"You know the agreement here, my little sewer rat. Turn around!"

Jeremy reluctantly turned his back to Carol so she could put the collar around his neck and lock it on. Most places, a bright blue dog collar with an electronic shocking device for training bird dogs might draw some looks, but in Key West on the eve of Fantasy Fest, it was hardly noticed.

With the number of people pouring onto the island, Carol was glad she'd spent the money on her new toy. She dropped the key down between her breasts, which were bunched up nicely from the designer bustier she wore, and showed Jeremy the little black box with the antenna.

"Supposed to have a range of two miles, which should work just fine here!" Carol gave an encouraging nudge. "Go on, act like you're going to slip away!"

Jeremy didn't seem to like the way things were going. He gave the collar a little test pull or two.

"And guess what! You can't cut that collar off, it's Kevlar with a titanium band inside. It's waterproof and virtually indestructible. This is so cool!" She nudged Jeremy again. "Go on! Make a break for it!"

Jeremy stayed real still, like he knew he was going to get it. Carol stuck the transmitter in her least favorite person's face.

"Look here, Jeremy! It even has an intensity control!" Carol regarded the little man standing very still, on his best behavior. "Oh well, I'm sure there'll be some opportunity to try it out. I'll just put it back in my bag here."

Carol saw the little man start to relax and mashed the button as hard as she could before dropping it in the bag. Jeremy screamed some unintelligible sound and grabbed his neck. People on the crowded sidewalk stared. Carol tried to look concerned, but couldn't stop laughing.

"It's okay, folks! He's just having one of his little fits! A little too much sun and he gets like this!"

Jeremy was red in the face and making gurgling sounds as she pushed him along to the end of Duval Street.

* * *

With Key West looking more like a city under siege by the hour, Carol realized the chances of finding one little mousy woman with two little gold statues were pretty slim. All they had to go on was someone using a stolen Spider Cult credit card for airfare to Key West on the same day Carol's Chacmools disappeared.

They walked by the former site of the Southernmost Marker, where there was a flurry of activity going on with dozens of workers building a huge raised stage.

It seemed that the upcoming Fantasy Fest parades, festivals, and benefit concert had flushed all the locals out of their usual hiding places. Besides the thousands of extra tourists, fishermen, bikers, and assorted oddballs, the streets were jammed with scruffy locals with tropical birds and big lizards hanging off their shoulders. They were riding rusty bicycles and driving beater cars whose only saving grace was their colorful paintjobs.

Carol and Jeremy walked by a couple of black people who seemed to be selling the last of their seashells to a throng of souvenir-hungry tourists. There was a woman sitting in the shade behind the shell stand with a shawl over her head holding an infant wrapped in an old blanket. The woman had her head down and seemed to be singing to the baby.

Carol had no idea how she was ever going to find Sara in this mess.

Chapter 40

Sara

Sara tried to relax, but she was still anxious. There were a lot of things she needed to know if she was going into the Everglades by herself to find the old treasure hunter Mr. Willie had told her about. She'd spent the evening before at the home of the two Willies, eating some fine food and listening to stories about boats and the sea. Along with the sea stories were some detailed instructions on navigation and boat engines.

They stayed up late, and when she finally got to sleep on the lumpy old couch, her dreams were of Charlie and the powerspot where the monument had been.

* * *

Willie had never seen Key West so busy. People were buying his shells at a record pace, and he hardly had time to think about much else, but he did. He thought about Sara and their talk the night before. At first, there were some serious doubts in his mind about a woman going into the Everglades by herself, but he soon realized this particular young woman was different. As they sat around a low table on the screened porch, he found her to be an excellent student, totally concentrated on everything he said.

"This be a chart. Shows this Key West and Keys here, and all this up here what they be calling Ten Thousand Islands and Everglades. They no cities at all in this whole area here. No stores, no roads, no houses, and no people even. They no bathrooms, neither."

Willie wanted to make it clear what this little woman was getting herself into. Sara just shrugged and kept looking at the chart. She asked all the right questions, and more than once he had to call on memories of experiences he hadn't thought about in years.

His grandson usually paid no mind to his stories, but he sat quietly the whole evening, learning about tides, wind, waves, the moon, and the sun. Maybe he was starting to grow up a little, or maybe he too could feel something in the air around this mysterious young woman with the two gold idols.

* * *

Sara was sitting in the shade behind the two shell merchants, anxiously thinking about her upcoming trip, when Carol and Jeremy walked by. She'd been expecting Carol to come after her, but it was still a shock to see the tall, shapely woman dressed like a lingerie model walking down the street twenty feet away with fat little Jeremy in tow. They didn't notice her sitting there; no one did.

Arrangements had been made the day before to rent a boat, and Willie was going to show Sara how to operate it after they closed up shop. Since it looked like they were going to be sold out of everything soon, the hands-on lessons might be starting early.

"You ready for a boat ride, little lady?" The senior Willie flashed a big smile full of gold. "It be a mighty fine-looking day! We get moving here, you might be getting on the water early enough to go on up today!"

Sara stood up and stretched. The tattered shawl went in a trash drum, so did the bundle of rags she'd been singing to. The two Willies seemed to be getting used to her strange ways and hadn't mentioned the disguise. She felt different, as well. Making decisions on her own after so many years gave her a weird feeling, kind of a sense of freedom.

The former Witchette was smiling from her head to her toes as she stood before her new friends.

"Mr. Willie." She bowed deeply to the old man. "And Mr. Willie." Another bow and a smile for the boy. "I would be delighted to go for a boat ride with you two gentlemen."

Sara put on a cloth hat and sunglasses from her bag and, again, looked like the most average of tourists. She hooked her arms through an arm of each of the Willies, and off they went toward the marina.

Chapter 41

Taco Bob Visits the West Coast

"Trout any way you can get 'em!"

After getting myself out of foggy-ass Cedar Key, I pointed my old truck south again and stopped a couple places along the west coast to check out the fishing.

I'd been curious about the Yankeetown area, so I went by and gave it a look. A long road came to a dead end right at a boat ramp on the Gulf next to a good-looking river. There were a couple of little islands in close and a channel going out through the flats. It was some prime-looking trout water. I was mighty tempted to throw the boat back in and give it a shot, but I wanted to stop by Orlando that evening since I was headed back around that part of the state.

Drove down south a little farther and checked out the Homosassa River, there where it goes out to the Gulf. It was getting to be that time of the year when fishermen from all over the world gather up there and go out after some of the biggest tarpon found anywhere in the state.

There was a TV on in the fishcamp tackle shop, and a handful of old-timers hanging around. The news was just ending, and the fellas were mostly trading opinions on the Southernmost Bandit while taking the occasional discreet pull on a Bush or Old Milwaukee beer they'd have stuck in a pocket or paper bag. A collection of shiny new pickups, rusty vans, and the occasional flashy sports cars sat patiently under old oaks that shaded the parking area.

A few boats had come back in from a day of fishing, and I talked to a couple guides cleaning some trout for their clients. Told me the trout and redfish were there, but were playing a little hard to get that day.

I noticed an ol' fella come up the river to the boat ramp in his boat. He seemed to be having a little trouble, so I went over to give him a hand. We got his boat up on the trailer and he drove the whole rig over in the shade. He thanked me and asked if I wanted a fish for my dinner. Judging by the looks of his old boat and motor, and ancient-looking fishing tackle, I didn't figure the poor ol' fella had much of any kind of fish, so I real polite-like turned down his offer.

"Suit yourself, I got plenty."

He opened up a beat-up old cooler strapped down in the front of his boat and I looked down at his limit of nice fat trout and a big redfish.

"Got this too!"

He reached down under the trout and pulled up a nice flounder. He wasn't done either.

"This makes some good stuffed flounder if you got any crabmeat for the stuffing." He took the piece of burlap cloth off a bucket. "Got that too!" He sure did, almost a full bucket of live blue crabs.

The old fella was enjoying the surprised look on my face. He took the biggest of the trout and wrapped it in some newspaper.

"I insist!" He handed it over and held up a hand when I tried to protest. "I done retired a few years ago. Just go out when the wife and me feel like a little seafood."

He showed me a popping float he used, and we talked trout bait a little before he headed out.

About the time I got done hanging around the fish-camp and talking fishing, it was getting dark, so I lit out for Orlando. I hoped Mary Ann would be glad to see me, even with showing up late, unannounced, and a little scruffy after spending the night sleeping in the sand out on an island.

* * *

They let me get a shower before we all sat down for the long version of the big, bald-headed guy who'd been by earlier. I was sitting with a couple of highly pissed-off young women that evening.

Mary Ann had come home just a little after the fella run off. She and her roommate worked at the same security outfit there in Orlando, mostly doing plainclothes security at ball games and concerts. The roommate's specialty was the dogs. They were used to dealing with people who felt the need to be assholes, but didn't at all like it happening where they lived. I gave it some hard thinking.

"Ladies, I got no earthly idea who might be looking for me. The only folks even know I was heading this way are the two Willies, Pete, and his sister. And any of them would have called here if anybody like Baldy came around asking about me."

At least we did have a good description to go on. We also had his gun. Mary Ann was going to see about getting the prints off the gun the next day, then maybe we'd have a name too.

From the story they told about the big shaved-head guy and the dog, I would imagine wherever he got off to he was a hurting son-of-a-bitch.

Chapter 42

Saul

Saul was hurting after his Orlando visit. Headed south and found a little hospital near the Everglades sugarcane fields. Just get a few stitches in the groin and hand, then maybe head over to Miami. Hole up for a couple of days.

Called in to LA the next morning, see if there was any news. Suits wanted to know if there was a problem on his end. He didn't need any grief from those people.

Couldn't believe he lost his gun. Just a throw-down with the numbers filed off, but still. Maybe let things settle a couple days in Orlando, then go back. Settle up with that dog and the woman both.

Chapter 43

Sara on the Water

Earlier in the morning, before the Governor's Key West press conference, Sara had bought everything on the list that Willie said she'd need for her trip into the swamp. The food and water items made sense, but she didn't understand why she needed four different kinds of mosquito repellent, mosquito netting, and a mosquito hood. Must be some mosquitoes where she was going.

* * *

The man at the boat rental place wasn't happy to see these people coming back to the marina. It was almost lunchtime and he was about to head out for a nice relaxing lunch after a hectic morning. He wasn't happy to see them because like everything else in Key West, the price of rental boats had gone up quite nicely after the Governor's press conference. The special four-day lobster season had brought the divers and fisherman in fast and hard. He'd already rented out all his boats for double the going rate and had a long waiting list.

"You folks going to go out for lobster?"

It was an odd group: an ancient black guy, a black kid wearing three ball caps and his underwear pulled up above his pants, and a quiet little white woman. What the hell, it was Key West.

The old guy gave him a look, but didn't say anything, just went straight over and got in the boat they'd picked out and paid for before the prices had gone up.

"You got them gas tanks filled up in this little scow like we talked about?" The old man hit the key and the motor started.

"Sure enough, partner! You sure you want to go out today? Lot of traffic out there with those lobster people now. If you want to change your mind on the rental, I'll be glad to give you your money back. No problem!"

He followed that up with his best salesman smile. The smiling stopped when the old guy waved the woman and kid aboard.

"Remember to have that boat back here by 5 pm day after tomorrow! There's a late charge after 5 pm!"

He started to mention stories of people falling out of rental boats and getting eaten by sharks, but the old fart was busy explaining things to the woman and wasn't paying him any attention. By the time his rental reached the far end of the marina, the woman was steering the boat.

* * *

There was a place they could pull the boat in on the other side of the island, not far from the home of the two

Willies. They got all of Sara's supplies and extra cans of gas loaded, and Willie went over some things on the boat one more time before he got out. With the waterproof chart taped to the console of the boat to guide her up to the mainland and the Ten Thousand Islands, Sara was alone in a boat for the first time in her life. She gave a little wave and a smile to the two figures watching her from the shore.

After a quick look around for other boats, she pushed the throttle all the way down. The skiff jumped up on a plane and was out of sight in a little over a minute.

Chapter 44

Carol and Jeremy

Mama Rosa, the palm reader, was doing a good business with all the extra people in town. She had an almost constant supply of eager tourists who wanted to be told that things were going to get better by a genuine Gypsy Far East Fortuneteller from Eastern Dayton.

It was an easy gig. Sit in the little room she rented in the back of a t-shirt shop, look at the Tarot cards, ask a few questions, and basically tell people what they wanted to hear.

The little bald man she'd made a sweet payday off once before was the next to come into the darkened room. Business was definitely looking up.

"Hey, Mama Rosa, remember me? You found a woman I was looking for a while back?"

The blue dog collar was new, but this was Key West, so she didn't ask. The former Ohio housewife let her eyelids droop and adjusted her numerous bracelets and rings.

"Yes," she said slowly in her best deep mysterious gypsy voice. "You are the one who seeks a little gold statue and pays with a little gold card."

This guy named Jeremy and some woman had been showing the picture of a missing gold statue around town before, and Mama Rosa knew a lot of people. The little man seemed impressed.

"Hey, that's right! Actually, we're looking for the same statue again."

He laid a picture of the idol on the table in front of Mama Rosa.

"In fact, we're looking for three of them this time, and we think this woman might know where they are."

A bad picture of a mousy woman went on the table next. Mama Rosa laid a hand on each picture and closed her eyes.

"Yes! She is near! I feel great mystery and danger!" She pulled her hands back off the pictures like they were burning. "There are strange forces at work here! I will have to consult the spirits to find this woman for you! This is too dangerous for me on my own!"

She closed her eyes while holding very still, then started making low moaning noises.

"So, Mama Rosa, how much is this going to cost anyway?"

Her eyes popped back open.

"Same deposit as last time, nonrefundable, cash or credit card, sorry no checks. Gimme a couple days."

The eyes slowly closed and the moaning started again. Jeremy filled out the form and came up with a shiny new Visa Gold.

* * *

The next day Mama Rosa's PI nephew in Miami, Tommy Areconda, came through with the news he had obtained through certain channels that there was a bounty hunter from Georgia subbing out some work for a big firm in LA. The nephew's source indicated one Saul Thorpe was contracted to find a certain unnamed fisherman who might have a little gold statue.

Tommy faxed his aunt in Key West the little bit of background info he had on Mr. Thorpe, and an invoice. His aunt was a little weirder than his other clients, but she was a good businesswoman and always paid her bills.

* * *

"She put her hand on the picture and said she's near! I think she's going to come through for us here, Carol!"

They were sitting on a low stone wall outside one of the outdoor cafés at the end of Duval Street. You could forget about getting a table, everything in Key West was filled to capacity and had been all day. A fat man with white hair and beard, wearing a rough sweater, was sitting at a table in the café with another fat guy who seemed to be painted gray. They were staring drunkenly at Carol, especially the part of Carol showing out of the top of her lacy bustier.

She wasn't impressed with what Jeremy had, but after a full day of fighting the crowds to get to the treasure museums around Key West, the former owner of two golden Chacmools didn't have anything better. No one recognized the picture of Sara she'd been showing around. Things looked bleak.

"Look, Carol, Mama Rosa said it would be a couple of days. What say we live a little while we're waiting?"

Jeremy was holding his hat in his lap and absently fingering himself while watching the women walking past. Carol was absently fingering the little controller in her bag. She was thinking about why she was sitting on a hard stone wall in Sweaty Pink Tourist Hell in the first place. Carol sighed, and her finger tapped the button.

Jeremy let out a yelp and both hands went to his neck. Hemingway gave Carol a lewd wink. Carol gave Papa the finger and turned slowly to Jeremy.

"Let's keep those hands where we can see them, my little perv." She waved the little black box menacingly. "How about I go somewhere and have a cool drink, and you sit here and look for your little friend Sara?"

Jeremy looked at Carol with pleading eyes.

"Okay, tell you what. You sit right here and look real hard while I'm gone, and maybe I'll bring you back some lemonade. How's that?"

Jeremy gave her a blank look. Carol slowly and deliberately put her finger on the button. The little man with the blue dog collar started panning his head back and forth, intently looking in the crowd of people passing by on the street. Jeremy and half the people in the café watched Carol's tight designer jeans walk back up Duval Street.

As soon as she was out of sight Jeremy ran into the cafe, forced his way through the crowd to the bar, and ordered a double Margarita, to go.

Chapter 45

Swamp

The trip to the Everglades coast didn't take as long as Sara thought it would. It was still a long ride though, and it was late afternoon by the time she got to what she hoped was the right area.

The water had gotten rough for part of the way, and she had to slow the boat down for the last hour of the trip to keep from getting pounded so much from the waves. Even with the charts it was tricky. Once she got to the mainland and started up Lost Man's River, there wasn't any chart of the area.

Going across Florida Bay from Key West had been all wide-open sky and water with the occasional little mangrove island. Going up the river it was a completely different world. She had seen a few other boats off in the distance earlier, but once up in the tree-shaded river she felt very alone.

There was nothing but mangrove trees here — huge trees that grew over the river and made darkness come early. The mangroves had shaded out all other vegetation — it was just mangroves, black water, and mosquitoes. The air smelled close and damp, with just a hint of decay.

Mr. Willie had been right about all that mosquito stuff. They were like a cloud that descended on her as soon as she got up into the dark shade of the river. The old man had said they were worse at night, so Sara got out the fine mesh net that covered her hat and came down to her shoulders. The only other place she had exposed skin was her hands, and the mosquitoes were already covering them. She sprayed repellent on her hands and some on her clothes as well.

Now all she had to do was travel the maze of little creeks and swamp that stretched for miles and find a little old hermit only one other person had seen in years. And find him before it got dark.

The creeks got narrower and shallower, and soon even with the motor idling and tilted up, it was hitting bottom. Sara turned the motor off and used the long pole that Willie had given her to push the boat slowly farther back in through the mangroves.

It was tough going in the steamy swamp — the skiff wasn't really built for poling.

Sara quickly learned to drink water from a plastic bottle without taking the mosquito net off her head. She just put the bottle to her mouth and drank through the screen. Having to pee was another matter.

There was no place to get out of the boat because there was no land. There was only black muck covered with several feet of tangled mangrove root. It was awkward enough trying to pee over the side of the boat. It didn't help that every mosquito for miles seemed to show up when her little white butt came out of her pants.

It stayed semi-dark for a long time, and then it got dark for real. Sara was quite a ways back in the swamp, so she tried calling out.

"Hello! My name is Sara! I am looking for the golden statue of the Chacmool! I don't mean any harm here! I come as a friend!"

The swamp was the darkest place she had ever seen. The trees covered what little light there was from the stars. The only sounds were the night birds in the distance and an occasional screeching noise she didn't think she wanted to know the source of. There were some frogs making noise and sometimes she heard something splashing in the water.

Mr. Willie had it right about the mosquitoes after dark too. For the first hour or so after sunset, they were worse than ever. Sara turned on her flashlight and scanned the area. She was amazed at how thick the cloud of mosquitoes had become. Even with two kinds of repellent on her hands she was getting bit. The thin gloves helped with the mosquitoes, but it was so hot and humid that Sara took the gloves back off after a while.

It was a still night, and Sara called out several more times. She hoped she was close enough to the old hermit that he would hear her and come to investigate. It was too dark to try poling anymore, so she tied the boat off to some mangrove roots and turned on the little lamp she had bought in Key West that morning.

The crowds of Key West, which she had experienced just that morning, seemed so unreal to Sara sitting there alone in the wilderness. Duval Street would be lit up with throngs of people for the first Fantasy Fest parade. Men and women in the parade would be wearing all kinds of wild costumes, there would be loud music coming from everywhere, and everyone would be drinking and yelling and acting crazy.

Surrounded by the pitch-black night, Sara opened a can of peaches under the little light in the boat. She managed to feed herself with out getting bit too many times and settled in for the night. It was too hot for the sleeping bag she'd brought, but it did make a nice sleeping pad on the front deck of the boat for her to curl up on.

She turned the light off and lay there listening to the night sounds and mosquitoes. In the morning she would find the old man and ask him for the third Chacmool. Then she wouldn't have to just dream about Charlie Spider anymore.

Chapter 46

Parade

It turned out Fantasy Fest wasn't so bad after all. Carol's everyday attire seemed to fit right in with the elaborate costumes and wild body paint most of the people were wearing. With a tall rum drink in her hand, she enjoyed the loud music and frenzied atmosphere of Duval Street while collecting an impressive amount of bead strings around her neck. Carol had to keep them arranged so they didn't cover too much cleavage, so she could get even more beads thrown to her from the floats in the parade.

The motel manager named André with whom she'd spent a lively evening in bed during her last stay in Key West recognized her and jumped off a float toward the end of the parade. He was a little drunk and seemed happy to see her, though he said he was a little wary of her since she'd kicked him out of her room at 3 am the last time. All the nearly naked sweaty bodies, music, and rum had Carol feeling very much a woman. She swore she wouldn't dream of kicking him out at 3 am again if he would like to stop by for a little while.

* * *

At 4 am sharp, Carol closed the door on a protesting André and went back to bed to get some sleep.

A little after eight she heard someone very carefully try the door to her room. There was just the slightest click as the lock held, then a faint scratching like someone using a credit card on the latch. After a quick glance at her watch, she sleepily reached into her bag by the bed and gave the little transmitter device a good squeeze. There was a loud scream outside the door followed by gagging sounds.

Carol fluffed her pillow a little before snuggling down into the bed and going back to sleep.

Chapter 47

Cabin

When Sara opened her eyes, there was just the faintest hint of daylight. The mosquitoes definitely seemed to be worst right at sunset and sunrise. She wanted to sleep more, but she needed to stick her butt over the side of the boat again. She stood and looked around in the pale light before quickly pulling down her pants and making the mosquitoes' day. After she had finished and mashed all the mosquitoes trapped in her pants, she looked around again slowly. It was very still in the swamp as the light tried to find its way through the mangrove canopy for another day.

She was about to try calling out again when there was movement in the distance. A small dark figure seemed to be standing on the water holding a long stick. She didn't move or make a sound, and the figure slowly came closer until she could see it was a person standing up and poling a little canoe that stuck up only a few inches above the water. There was hardly a ripple of water from the canoe as it eased closer, and not a sound.

"Hello, my name is Sara! I'm looking for a man who might be a treasure hunter. I am seeking a gold statue, a little idol called a Chacmool."

The canoe stopped far enough away that Sara still couldn't make out what the little man looked like in the semi-darkness. She carefully reached down into her bag, pulled out a Chacmool, and held it over her head.

"I am looking for one of these!"

The canoe came closer. Sara slowly brought the idol down and held it out toward the approaching figure. As he got closer she could see that it wasn't an old man at all, but a young boy, maybe ten or twelve years old. He seemed to have some Indian features, but it was hard to tell in the poor light, and because he was wearing a large hat and old baggy clothes. He seemed to be looking at the idol, not at her.

When he got close enough, the boy reached out, took the Chacmool, and held it close to his chest to examine it. He was near now, but she still couldn't see his face because of the hat. The small hands of the boy brought the idol back toward her, and she noticed that he was missing the little finger on his left hand. The boy was smiling and Sara started to smile back, then she saw his eyes. Sara felt a flash of alarm and almost dropped the idol in the water. It was the face of a young boy, but the gleaming eyes were those of an old man.

* * *

After a couple of hours of poling the skiff behind the boy and his canoe, Sara was working up a good sweat. The coolness of the morning hadn't lasted long, and she had to pole hard to keep up with the boy. There were some breaks in the tree canopy that let in some sunlight, and the mosquitoes didn't seem to be as bad. At least she didn't need the netting over her hat anymore.

He hadn't said a word after handing the idol back to her, just gave her a smile and started to pole his canoe back from where he'd come. He hadn't gone far when he turned and motioned for her to follow. His little log canoe seemed to slip effortlessly through the mangrove swamp, while Sara was having a hard time with the much larger and heavier skiff.

Once, after a quick drink of water, Sara didn't see the boy out ahead anymore. She poled along a little further before stopping and looking all around. At first she didn't see it in the distance, but there seemed to be a roof outline in the trees, and then she saw the boy sitting in front of a doorway smiling and waving.

"Is this your home? Where are your parents?"

Sara tied the skiff to the wooden steps in front of the weathered little cabin stuck back in the mangroves. Inside the screen door was a small table and a rusty little stove. There was a mat on the floor against the far wall and different kinds of dried roots hanging by strings from the ceiling rafters. A small stack of old paperback books was against the wall not far from the stove, the book on top of the pile missing most of its pages. She figured the book pages were being used to start fires. There was a black iron pot on the stove with some kind of soup. The soup smelled really good.

"Do you live here by yourself?"

The boy pointed to the table, where there was a box to sit and a wooden bowl and spoon. Sara got the picture and helped herself to some soup. It was different than anything she'd had before, but it was warm and delicious.

"This is good stuff! Did you make this yourself?"

The boy sat against the wall on the floor not far from the mat. He smiled at his guest and then looked to his left, toward the mat, nodded, and let out a quick little laugh. He almost seemed to be carrying on a conversation with someone else, an invisible person. Great, thought Sara, and I'm the one people are always saying is a little crazy. The boy suddenly turned to her and tilted his head to one side and smiled. His strange eyes were full of mischief.

"I am Henry. I thought you might want to get out of the bugs for a while. Maybe have some soup?"

He looked over at his imaginary friend again, and looked surprised and put his hand over his mouth to suppress a laugh. Sara kept eating; she hadn't realized how hungry she was. The boy seemed to get over his joke with his invisible friend.

"I'm sorry, I don't mean to be rude. I don't get many visitors."

He was sitting up straight now and giving Sara his full attention.

"My parents are long gone, but do not worry about that. I am fine here by myself." He seemed to be trying to ignore something going on to his left and gave a quick little smile that way. "I'm quite curious about the little statue you have. Did you say you were looking for one like it?"

Sara stopped eating. This was what she had come for.

"Yes, I have two, and I am looking for the third one. An old black man in Key West told me that someone he knows was back here not long ago and met an old man who used to hunt for buried treasure on the islands. For some reason I thought he might have it."

The young boy nodded, then shook his head.

"There used to be a little statue here like the one you have, but it is gone."

Sara's disappointment must have showed. The boy looked to his left, then back at his guest and smiled.

"I wouldn't be surprised if it came back again sometime soon though."

Chapter 48

Chacmools

The days Sara spent with the young boy were some of the most interesting of her life. Henry took her around the swamp and introduced her to some of his friends. Further inland the terrain changed, with more types of vegetation and wildlife. There were palms to rattle in the breeze and, in the water, logs with eyes that turned out to be alligators. Sara had trained for years to be quiet, and could stalk most animals and people with ease, but she was a clumsy mess compared with little Henry. He could move through the woods in a way that didn't even disturb the leaves on the ground.

The friends turned out to be a deer and some raccoons. When they went to a place where there was some dry land and a vegetable garden, a small doe came out of the brush after the boy made a purring sound. Sara had never been so close to wild animals before, but the boy and the deer seemed so natural together that she didn't even flinch when the deer came over to her and put its head under her hand so she would scratch it.

Sara didn't even notice the heat or the bugs, and then she wondered if she might be dreaming the place with the deer and vegetable garden. She looked at the hand that wasn't scratching the deer and counted her fingers. Five was right, it wasn't a dream.

Henry was working in the garden, pulling weeds and talking to his imaginary friend. The deer turned its head and Sara looked back over at the boy, but now there were two boys. Startled, she looked back at the deer. The deer's eyes seemed to glow before it slipped back into the brush with hardly a sound.

The two boys were wearing nearly identical dirt-colored clothes and sitting on the ground side by side in the shade near the garden. They were quietly watching her as she came over and sat in front of them. She looked at the new boy sitting to the left of Henry and felt a sudden shiver of fear. Thinking she must surely be dreaming this time, Sara started to raise her hand up to count the fingers, but the new boy put his hand over hers. Henry gave her a serious look.

"There is no need for this. It does not matter here if you are dreaming or not, it only matters that you can see him now."

The new boy was definitely Indian, about the same age and size as Henry, but with a rounder, flatter face and long black hair. His eyes were scaring her; they were even older eyes than Henry's — ancient eyes. Sara couldn't look away from the new boy's eyes; her body was afraid and wanted to flee.

Just as she about to jump up and run for her life, the new boy smiled for the first time and started to chant real low. Henry picked up on it and started humming a tune that somehow went with what the other boy was chanting. Almost immediately she calmed down. Soon the strange tune had words, and the two boys ended up singing a funny song about a raccoon that liked to steal bird eggs but was always falling out of trees.

The song ended and Sara wondered at how she had gone from panic to laughing about the silly song in such a short time. Henry saw it when she started getting nervous again.

"Please excuse my friend, Sara. He is really quite harmless —"

To prove his point, Henry gave the other boy a good shove. Without moving his arms or legs, the boy fell over onto his side. The momentum rolled him further, until he was balancing on his head with his legs still crossed in a sitting position. Sara was spellbound at the acrobatic feat.

"— although he is a bit of a show-off sometimes."

Henry gave the Indian boy another push. This time he rolled around on the ground, then partway up a tree trunk, before rolling back and sliding up next to Henry.

"Sara meet Newt; Newt, this is Sara."

Newt sprang to his feet, bowed deeply, gently took Sara's hand in his, and gave it a quick kiss before falling backwards and landing in a sitting position next to Henry.

"His real name is Nutehamomoiki, but I just call him Newt for short."

The boy called Newt gave Sara a grin so big she thought he might be about to pull a muscle in his face.

"I think Newt would like to tell you about his people, but sometimes he is a little shy and can't seem to talk to strangers."

Newt nodded his head vigorously to agree with what Henry was saying, then made some grotesque contortions with his mouth like he was trying to talk but couldn't. He seemed to be having a lot of trouble, grunting and making terrible noises, and looked truly to be trying as hard as he could to talk. Henry looked at his friend and rolled his eyes.

"He's like this sometimes. He'll talk when he's ready."

Newt was grabbing at his lips and making horrible sounds. Sara didn't know whether to laugh or run. The boy was giving her a pleading look, like he wanted her to help him. He kept struggling and pointed to his back and started to hiccup. His hiccups grew so strong that he was bouncing off the ground each time. Henry started to laugh. Newt was frantically pointing at his back and imploring Sara with his eyes to help him.

"What is wrong with him? What does he want me to do?"

The boy's hiccups were becoming so violent he was coming off the ground almost a foot each time. Henry was holding his side and laughing.

"I think he wants you to pound on his back, Sara. He seems to have something stuck inside that is keeping him from speaking."

Sara jumped up and ran behind the bouncing, hiccupping boy and gave him a good shot between the shoulder blades. The blow knocked the boy forward and he ended up balanced on his head in a sitting position again.

Newt had stopped hiccupping and making noises, and stayed balanced on his head for several seconds before releasing a long, loud fart.

Henry was rolling on the ground laughing. Newt toppled down and started laughing just as hard. Sara wondered what the hell she had gotten herself into for a second, then started laughing herself.

After the two boys had composed themselves and taken their places sitting on the ground, Henry gave Newt a stern look and turned to Sara.

"My friend here does have a lot of things he would like to tell you, and show you." Henry looked to his left and the other boy gave him a look of angelic innocence. "If he can control himself for a while that is."

Newt now looked determined, almost fierce. Sara felt safe with these two strange boys, but on guard. She decided to go for the big question.

"What do you know about the Chacmools, Newt?"

* * *

Newt could talk all right, and once he got started he had a lot to say. Sara learned of his people, the People of the Chacmools.

"In the first days there were several sets of the Golden Chacmools and many of my people. My people spent countless generations perfecting lucid dreaming and their dreaming bodies. Since ancient times the parents would remove the small finger on the left hand of their babies at birth. It was a mark of my people, so that we could always identify one another. Dreaming bodies are always perfect replicas of the dreamer, except without any physical imperfections, so the dreaming bodies of my people had all their fingers."

Sara looked at Newt's hands, and saw that he had all his fingers. She was amazed to see that Henry did also.

"The Chacmool's power was coveted and sometimes abused by others. Wars were fought. Over the centuries many people and nearly all of the Chacmools were destroyed or lost by the greed and ignorance of those seeking the Spirit Idol's power.

"My people were the guardians of the Chacmools. We traveled freely between the world of man and that of the spirits of the earth. As the greed of man took its toll on the Spirit Idols, my people also became fewer and less powerful. Those who survived to modern times were not much more than observers, with barely enough power to stay in the world of men for short periods of time.

"It was one of my people, the People of the Chacmools, who helped a shaman hide one of the idols from the Spanish, the same idol that a man named Charlie Spider had bought at a small village market over two hundred years later."

Sara asked how many sets of the Chacmools were left, and the strange Indian boy held up one finger. She was almost afraid to ask — she felt she already knew the answer — but she asked how many People of the Chacmools were left. There was sadness in the eyes of both boys as Newt again held up one finger.

* * *

Sara followed the two boys as they walked through the wilderness. They showed her wild birds and animals that she never would have noticed on her own. She saw wild boar, several more deer, and large white birds looking for an easy meal along the edge of the water while trying to avoid becoming a meal themselves for a hungry alligator. There were little snakes and turtles by the water, and songbirds in the trees.

The boys showed her how to walk so that she wouldn't disturb the Earth Mother as she traveled upon her surface. It was difficult at first to concentrate on holding her fingers a certain way while not looking just at what was directly in front of her, but at everything in her field of vision. After a while, though, she was able to move almost as silently through the woods as her young guides.

Newt mimicked someone stumbling through the woods looking up at the trees and stepping on a snake and messing his pants. His pantomime was so perfect and his look of horror at stepping on a snake so hilarious that they had to stop for several minutes until their laughter subsided before they continued.

Though Sara had learned about wild plants and their uses when she was in tracker school, there were many types of vegetation here that she had never seen before. The boys would stop from time to time to point out a plant that was good to eat, a vine to drink clear water from, or a tree with bark that could be made into medicine. All the plants, animals, and insects, the sun, sky, and breeze flowed together for Sara in a way that she had never experienced. Everything seemed to move in an entirely predictable way, and the sounds of the wilderness were almost like a long soothing melody. There was so much to know, so much to learn. Sara became overwhelmed and dizzy. She had to rest.

When she sat down on the ground she immediately felt better. She looked for the boys, but saw only Henry. He was sitting close by, where she had seen him before by the little garden. She then noticed it was nearly dark, and the mosquitoes were getting bad again.

"Where has Newt gone?"

Henry looked to his left and shrugged his shoulders. He gave Sara a wink.

"Let's get a few vegetables for some soup. Maybe he will come to the cabin later." Henry stood and stretched like he had been sitting for a long time. Sara stood and realized that even though she had just sat down, for some reason she felt as though she had been sitting for hours.

Henry was digging up some little carrots and potatoes from the sandy soil. He handed them to Sara to put in her bag for the trip back to the cabin. She noticed in the dim light that the boy was again missing the small finger on his left hand.

* * *

After they had eaten their fill of the delicious soup in the little cabin, Sara sat on the mat and Henry took his usual place nearby along the wall. The constant buzz of mosquitoes that covered the screens and the occasional call of a night bird were the only sounds. A small fire in the cooking stove cast long gray shadows through the room.

"Where has Newt gone, Henry? I wanted to ask him more about the Chacmools."

Henry looked to his left and winked.

"He is still here. If you want to see him, just let your thoughts go to sleep and stay awake. Understand?"

Sara was anxious, and a little apprehensive, to see and talk to the phantom boy again. She had trouble quieting her mind, but finally the familiar calm came and slowly washed her thoughts away. Everything became clearer, and she could see inside the cabin as though it were daylight. She could see everything in the room in minute detail, almost as though magnified.

Henry was sitting on his spot, still with a big smile and those old man's eyes. Instinctively, Sara brought her hand up to check her fingers. As soon as she did, something black flew in front of her just missing her face. She yelped and jumped back, hitting her head against the wall behind her.

There were two boys now, both rolling on the floor, overcome with spasms of laughter. Henry sat up and was wiping away tears.

"I'm sorry, Sara. Newt gets a little carried away with his tricks sometimes. You'll have to forgive him. He doesn't get many chances to clown around with others."

Sara was rubbing the back of her head. She had really gotten a good whack, and it hurt. It came to her that if Newt wasn't always clowning around, she probably wouldn't be able to be around him. As awesome as he had been out in the wilderness during the day, he seemed to be even more powerful at night. The air around Newt seemed to almost glow with energy like an electrical charge.

Sara tried to fight it, but she could feel her fear building. It was beyond any sort of rational thing, more a primal feeling. Her body's warning systems were at full alert.

The two boys sat side by side, staring at her. Their eyes were like pools of black liquid. Sara's mind filled with raw terror, and she could feel a scream coming from deep inside. Newt was suddenly in front of her, grabbing her head in his hands and turning it to the left. Something in her neck popped, and she wasn't in the little cabin out in the Everglades swamp anymore.

* * *

It was an immense room with a very high ceiling. Everything seemed to be made of white stone, and the huge room was brightly lit, though Sara didn't notice the source of the light. In the center of the room were several large men who appeared to be guards, with sword-like weapons and long spears. They wore brightly colored robes and fierce-looking masks shaped like a jaguar's head. There was a raised area like a large bed, which seemed to be what the men were guarding. Someone was lying on the bed.

Sara looked around and found Newt standing next to her. She was no longer afraid of him, instead she felt great affection and trust toward him

Newt put his index finger to his lips to signal her to be quiet, then pointed to the bed where the figure was lying. Sara moved closer and could see it was a woman lying on her back, with a golden Chacmool by each ear and another over her eyes. There was a shimmer of energy in the air around the woman, similar to what she had experienced with Newt in the cabin.

Something about the dark-haired woman caused Sara to look closer at her face. There was something across the woman's mouth, a gold piece of cloth or a scarf. Sara looked at Newt, who gave an almost imperceptible nod toward the woman on the bed. She reached out and carefully lifted the cloth from the woman's mouth. The woman was smiling, and Sara suddenly felt something was wrong. Before she could put the cloth back across the woman's mouth, she grabbed Sara's hand and held it with an incredibly strong grip. Sara tried to free herself as the woman's other hand reached for the Chacmool that covered her eyes. Sara started to wail and frantically pulled to get away before the woman took the idol away from her eyes. The Chacmool came away and the eyes opened, staring directly at Sara. The woman looked exactly like Carol. Sara screamed.

* * *

Everything was wet. Sara was sitting on the steps of the little cabin and the two boys were pouring buckets of water over her. She shook her head, then her whole body, like a dog drying itself off. A feeling of calm and strength came over her. She held up her hand.

"Enough!"

Newt had a bucket of water poised over her head. He shrugged, then poured the whole bucket over her head. Sara had been about to say something else and got a mouthful of swamp water. She sputtered and coughed, then pointed at Newt.

"You!"

She made a grab and just missed as the boy yelped and jumped away. Sara was on her feet, and the chase was on. Henry fell back against the cabin laughing. It wasn't a long chase, since there were only a few square feet of wood planking surrounded by a few hundred acres of shallow water and swamp. Sara had Newt by the back of the collar, dragging him struggling and laughing back to the front of the cabin, where she grabbed a bucket of water and thoroughly soaked him.

* * *

Wearing clean, dry clothes from her boat, Sara sat in the cabin with the two boys again. She wanted to ask about the vision of the Chacmools, but fell asleep on the mat.

When she woke, both boys were still sitting there, just as they had been before she slept. It was late morning.

"What was that place, Newt? And why was Carol there?"

The boys continued to look at her without moving for several seconds. Although Sara trusted the boys explicitly, she still felt a little apprehensive with the two of them staring at her. Sometimes they didn't seem like young boys at all.

Newt took a deep breath and exhaled through his lips, making a strange sound.

"Something happened there, Sara. I wanted you to see the Temple of the Chacmools, but I didn't think you could pierce the dream."

Newt stared at Sara with his big black eyes. She stared back.

"But what is that place? Is it a place that existed in the past? And what do you mean by 'pierce the dream'?"

Newt seemed to have something in his hand. He looked at the other boy before answering.

"The place we went to doesn't exist in what you would normally think of as time. It is just there, as it has always been. There is always someone, usually a woman, on the Temple bed with the Chacmools."

Newt appeared nervous for the first time since she'd met him. His nervousness was contagious, and Sara was hanging on his every word.

"You pierced the dream when you took the scarf from the face of the woman. I know of the person you call Carol, but I had never seen the face of anyone in the temple before and was shocked myself to see her there. I have no idea what it means.

"Everything changed when you pierced the dream. The guards were about to grab us both when Henry dragged you outside the cabin and poured water on you. You can scream really loud, you know."

Newt smiled and some of the tension was broken, but Sara was still on edge.

"But it was just a dream, right? You said it was a dream!"

Newt's smile faded as he opened his hand.

"Not a dream anymore," he dropped a gold scarf on the floor in front of them. "You brought this back with you."

Chapter 49

Carol

Carol lounged in bed for a while, thinking about the weird dream she'd been having before the roar of a navy jet taking off from the base nearby woke her up. She had strange dreams from time to time, but this one had been a real doozy.

The events of the evening before started coming back to her as she lay there. The crazy parade in town, the rum, the music, and the guy who was manager of a motel there on the island. What was his name? André, that was it. A perfectly manicured finger absently worked its way up a nostril as the Head Witchette of the Spider Cult sighed and thought about the man that had been in her bed a few hours earlier.

As she woke up a little more, Carol started remembering details of her wild night of uninhibited passion. There was a strange and rather unpleasant taste in her mouth, and Carol suddenly cringed at the memory of something she'd done. She jumped out of bed and ran to the bathroom. After gargling a large glassful of mouthwash, she spent several minutes thoroughly brushing her tongue.

* * *

After a relaxing lunch in the hotel restaurant, Carol allotted a few minutes of her time to wondering about Jeremy. She made sure not to give him too much money at a time so he wouldn't hurt himself too badly, and took her credit card back after the fortune teller had been paid.

Jeremy hadn't been outside her door when she'd gone to lunch. Carol was a little concerned about him. She didn't want anything bad to happen to the person who had caused her to lose two-thirds of what she needed to have anything she wanted in the whole world, forever. Jeremy needed to stay reasonably healthy until she had all three Chacmools, since she might need someone to try out her new powers on. A couple of quick taps on the transmitter in her bag would let him know she was thinking about him. Maybe give the little weasel a call when she got back to her room.

Carol's thoughts drifted back to the details of the previous night. She picked up a handful of breath mints on her way out of the restaurant.

* * *

"Hello?"

"Just thought I'd call and see how you were doing."

"Shit, Carol! You think you could lay off the collar a little? I just mashed a jelly donut all over my new tropical shirt! I could have hurt myself bad if you did that while I was shaving!"

"Poor Jeremy, I'm just sooo sorry. What time do you usually shave?"

"Very funny, Carol. You're a real laugh riot."

"I want you to get your chubby little ass over to Old Town and see if your fortune teller has anything for us yet."

"She said it would be a couple of days. Besides there's something coming up on the Food Channel that..."

There was a quick gasp and choking sounds. Carol put the little transmitter back in her bag.

"What's that, Jeremy? There seems to be something wrong with the connection here."

"I, uh, said I'll head over there right away, my Queen."

Carol didn't really like Jeremy's tone of voice, but decided to let it pass.

"Give me a call as soon as you talk to her. I'll be waiting."

She stretched out on the bed and found the Food Channel on the television.

"Oh gross! It's the one about eels!"

She held the remote up to change channels, then relented and watched the entire show repulsed, but thoroughly captivated.

Chapter 50

The Boys

Despite Sara's asking several times, neither boy would talk about the Temple. Instead, they spent the day showing her more of the fascinating wilderness surrounding the cabin. She soon forgot her concerns and was once again caught up in witnessing the flow of life with her two guides.

It was a tight fit, but all three of them went in the little dugout canoe. Henry stood in the back and poled them east for miles through the swamp, and then when the terrain changed, they went up narrow channels. Henry was pointing out things to Sara, sitting with Newt in the bottom of the canoe.

"This is far enough. From here the water goes only a short distance more. In the dry months, there is a path that goes to an Indian store along the highway. There are some houses there where people live."

Sara listened carefully and thought she could hear road noise off in the distance.

She thoroughly enjoyed being out in the wild with the two boys. She gained an appreciation and knowledge of the Everglades in the short time she spent with her hosts that would have taken her years to acquire on her own.

That evening, Sara was instructed in the making of the mysterious soup. She had expected an extensive process bordering on ritual to make such fine-tasting soup, and hoped her own cooking expertise would help her grasp the finer points.

Newt lit a candle and then laid the vegetables they had brought from the garden on the table. Earlier, he'd watched Sara carefully wash them in water from the rain barrel.

After the vegetables were laid out to his liking, he took one of the dried tubers that hung from the rafters. He softly chanted while carefully removing some cobwebs and the string that had held it in place. He laid it on the wooden table with the vegetables and passed his hands palms down over the table several times. The chanting became louder. His eyes were closed.

Suddenly Newt reached up to a shelf along the wall and with a flick of his wrist an old paring knife landed blade-first on the table and stuck there. His eyes slowly opened. He stared at Sara and pointed his finger at her without missing a beat in his chanting. Sara never took her eyes from Newt. She pulled the blade out of the table and held it in her hand, ready for whatever. Newt's chanting suddenly stopped.

Sara had never heard a voice so low, or so loud. The voice that came out of the boy seemed to shake the little cabin.

"Now you must cut the sacred vegetables!"

Newt's voice startled her so bad she took her eyes off him for a second and glanced at the other boy. Henry had his hand over his mouth like he was about to explode with laughter. When she looked back at Newt, he was sitting cross-legged on top of the vegetables right in front of her.

The shock of seeing the boy suddenly only inches away caused her to fall back off the box she was sitting on. Somehow Henry had gotten around in time to catch her before she hit the floor. The two boys were in hysterics. She stared at them dumbfounded, which just seemed to prolong their spasms of laughter. Henry finally caught his breath.

"Don't feel too bad, Sara. He did something like that to me once."

He gave Newt a stern look. Newt looked the picture of innocence, sitting on the table wiping his eyes.

"At least he didn't make you take off all your clothes and get 'purified' with swamp water first."

Newt got another stern look.

"Actually, all we do is cut up whatever we have and add some spices and other things," he held up the gnarled little tuber. "If Newt will leave you alone for a few minutes, I would appreciate it if you would go ahead and make up the soup. I, for one, am getting hungry."

He handed her a jar of powder from the shelf.

"Put a pinch or two of this in there too."

He gave her a wink and went out into the darkness, followed closely by Newt. She could hear whispering and muffled laughter coming from the front steps as she prepared the soup.

Later that evening Sara sat on her usual place on the mat, and the boys sat on the floor facing her. She was beginning to feel more comfortable with them, despite their clowning and mystery. The boys were restless, squirming around, and couldn't seem to sit still. Something was up. Newt made a show of clearing his throat.

"I told you things had changed since you pierced the dream."

This was the first mention of the Temple dream all day. Sara leaned forward and cocked her head slightly, her eyes locked on Newt.

"You probably noticed."

The boy held up his left hand. Sara had noticed, but hadn't said anything. The little finger on Newt's hand was missing.

"We've felt for a while now that something was going to happen here, so we've been getting ready." Both boys smiled and fidgeted. "There's no way for us to know what it means or how long it will last, so we've decided to leave."

The boys were so excited they could hardly hold still and for once were really acting like young boys. Sara's perplexed look sent them into a short giggle fit. She couldn't for the life of her imagine where two young boys living in the swamp dressed in rags would be going.

"Where will you go? What will you use for money?"

The boys were obviously ready for her questions. They each pulled large stacks of bills from their clothes and fanned them out like a deck of cards on the floor. There was a lot of money there, maybe thousands of dollars. Sara's jaw dropped at the sight of all that money. The grinning boys had an announcement as well.

"We're going to Disney World!"

Henry and Newt began pulling more money from their clothes and throwing it in the air. They jumped to their feet and ran laughing out the door. As the money floated down to the floor, Sara thought, at least there wasn't ever a dull moment with these two.

Sara scooped up the money and put it in a pile along the wall. There really was an impressive amount of cash. She heard a noise and looked up to see Henry, then Newt come through the door. Her mouth dropped open again as she stared at the transformation. Both boys were wearing brand new clothes that looked like the latest fashion. They were both sporting designer backpacks, and Newt was wearing headphones. He was listening to a CD and bobbing his head. Both boys looked like they had just stepped off the set of the latest MTV commercial.

With deadly serious expressions, each boy took a few steps toward Sara and slowly turned like fashion models on a runway. Newt reached down to Sara sitting on her mat and gently pushed her chin up to close her mouth. He slipped the headphones on her head for her to hear — it was chanting, the same chanting he had been doing earlier with the vegetables. He took the headphones back and sat on the floor in front of her next to Henry. Both boys were grinning from ear to ear. Sara shook her head to clear it.

"You guys are too much! So now you're going to Disney-world? You've got clothes. You've got money."

It dawned on her that they really were going to leave her. She felt crummy that her first thought was for herself, when she should be happy for them.

"But how will you get there? You'll need an adult to go with you, or else they'll never let you in."

Newt nodded his head.

"There is a man who lives not far from the store we told you about. The man has not lived there long. He takes care of sick and injured animals at his house. We are his friends, and he will take us." Sara started to say something, but Henry held up his hand.

"He is quite a good man, Sara, and has helped us with our financial matters recently. You see, there really was an old treasure hunter living here at one time." Henry gave the other boy a quick wink. "Our friend was taught accounting by an Asian gentleman and has helped us sell some of the treasure discreetly. He is a large, gentle man and a great friend to us. Perhaps you have heard of him? His name is Horatio Bloomer, but he likes to be called Horse."

Sara had never heard of anyone named Horse before.

"No, sorry." She looked at the two amazing boys sitting in front of her in their new clothes, in an old cabin in the middle of a tropical swamp miles from anyone or anything. "It does look like you've got things thought out pretty thoroughly."

"These clothes came from Miami, our friend bought them for us several days ago."

Newt's eyes went wide. "Almost forgot! We also have credit cards!" He pulled out a wallet and proudly held up a shiny new American Express.

Henry worked his eyebrows up and down provocatively and took out a card of his own. "Gold card!" He stuck his nose up a little and slowly panned the card for Sara and Newt to see.

Newt was not about to be outdone and pulled out another card, holding it up triumphantly.

"Platinum!"

Sara couldn't believe these two guys. Henry frantically dug through every fold in his wallet. He stopped and slowly produced a silver card.

"Titanium!"

He gave the other boy a smug, self-satisfied look. Sara looked at Newt.

Newt made a big production of going through his wallet and pockets. He finally pulled something from the bottom of his backpack and held it up. The card actually glowed in the dim light of the cabin.

"Plutonium! When only the very best will do!"

The nightbirds and raccoons in the swamp were the only ones awake to hear the laughter coming from the cabin.

Chapter 51

Taco Bob, the Chef

"It's all in the presentation!"

I spent a couple of days hanging out and resting up at Mary Ann's in Orlando. It was too late, and the women were too upset from the guy trying to bust into the apartment, for any fish cooking the first night. The next day we cooked up that big trout the ol' fella in Homosassa gave me. It was mighty fine.

* * *

Whole Baked Trout

One nice size trout, head and all
One large orange, sliced
Cajun seasoning

Clean out the trout real good (remove the innards and gills), and scrub the scales clean with a brush.

Make some little cuts on the outside of the fish and squeeze a little orange juice over the whole thing.

Stuff the body cavity with orange slices and give the fish a little Cajun seasoning all over.

Wrap loosely in aluminum foil and place in a cooking pan.

Check with a fork after baking at 350 for 30 minutes or so. Might take an hour if it's a real big fish.

If you want to get fancy, you can throw a few sprigs of parsley on there before serving, and maybe even a topwater plug in the mouth for that great first impression when you put it on the table.

Chapter 52

Taco Bob Goes Back to the Swamp

"Always time for a little trout fishing!"

Heading down to Chokoloskee to do some trout fishing was as good an excuse as any to go check on old Mr. Small down in the Ten Thousand Islands. It was the next place I had planned to go on my trout tour of Florida.

Turns out the security outfit Mary Ann and her roommate worked for was sending them down to Key West for a few days to work the big benefit concert coming up with Marty the Manatee. Mary Ann was a big fan of Marty's music, and she jumped at the chance to take the job.

The roommate was driving down to the Keys with one of her dogs, and Mary Ann was riding with me over to Chok. The plan was to put the boat in there at Chok so I could do a little fishing and pay a visit to the old man up in the swamp. Mary Ann would drive my old truck with the boat trailer on down to Key West, and I'd just head on down there in my boat after I got in enough fishing and visiting.

It was about as fine-looking a day as you could ask for as me and Mary Ann made the drive over to the southwest coast. We got out of Orlando before the morning rush, and Mary Ann had some Marty the Manatee songs going on her CD player. Pretty soon we were singing along and laughing at ourselves. After singing "Tequila Breakfast" too many times, we naturally had to have a Tequila Sunrise with our lunch once we got to the restaurant there in Chok.

There was a fella with a big mustache at the marina where we put the boat in, who was looking us over pretty good. I figured he was just checking out Mary Ann, but after she left with the truck for the Keys, he came over to talk.

"You the same guy come in a while back pulling them folks in with the broke-down boat, ain't ya?"

I gave him a good look. He was the one I seen working there before. Good-sized fella, seemed all right. I didn't say anything, but gave him a little bit of smile.

"I ain't meaning to be nosy about your business, but the cops come by asking questions about those folks you dropped off, then some big shaved-head guy was here a few days ago asking about the fisherman that pulled them folks in."

This here was all news to me. I wasn't too surprised to find out the police would be asking about the folks I pulled in that day. No telling what they'd been up to, 'cause they sure didn't look like they knew what they were doing out on the water.

The big shaved-head guy looking for me was interesting, and I wished I'd known a few minutes earlier so I could have told Mary Ann before she left. I thanked the guy for the information and asked him where there was a phone I could use. I called Mary Ann's cell phone and told her the latest on Saul Thorpe.

Mary Ann's roommate had gotten the prints off the gun run down through a friend at work. The big shaved-head guy who had tried to force his way into the apartment, before Fluffy did her impression of a crotch-sniffer, was some kind of bounty hunter from Georgia. They were hoping to get more information sent down to Key West when it came in. We all wanted to have a word or two with Mr. Thorpe from Georgia.

* * *

It looked like the weather was going to hold as I left out of the marina at Chokoloskee on the start of a good incoming tide. Light wind, not too hot, a few puffy white clouds, and the usual one or two small planes droning away in the bright blue sky.

Since I was in a boat full of fishing and camping supplies, a little trout fishing seemed like a good idea. I ran down the coast a ways and found some nice-looking grass flats in about three feet of water. I came up with some baitfish with the cast net and set a pinfish out to soak off the back of the boat on one pole while I was throwing a plastic-tailed jig. I just drifted with the tide for a while and picked up the usual assortment of aerobatic ladyfish, small trout, and mean-ass little sharks. A three-foot blacktip shark was the last thing the little pinfish on the float saw, and I fought the shark for a while on the bigger pole before I got him up close to the boat.

That little shark put me in mind of the huge Hammerhead that had pulled Mr. Small out of the boat when he was with me that time. The old man had been trying to get the hook out of the mouth of a big Tarpon, and the shark had come from up under the boat and grabbed the tarpon's head and

Mr. Small's hand. The old man lost a finger, but it could have been a lot worse. Ever since that day I had a real healthy respect for sharks. Little ones, but especially big ones.

That little blacktip wasn't acting like he was going to let me try to take the hook out of his mouth without trying to do me some damage, so I cut the line and let him have the hook as a little souvenir to remind him of his encounter with Taco Bob.

The whole coast along that part of the state is nothing but miles of mangrove trees. Everything looks about the same as it did back in the Indian days, since the National Park folks took out just about any man-made thing except a few channel markers for the bigger rivers. Enough of a breeze kicked up the waves to where standing up in the boat without falling in was a challenge, so I ran on down to the mouth of Lost Man's River. Got myself set up with a live bait on the big pole drifting out back of the boat while I worked on a Cuban sandwich.

Nothing was interested in my bait off the back, so I used the trolling motor I'd put on the boat before I left Key West to ease on up the river and make a few casts with a topwater plug. Mr. Small had been with me once on that river showing me some places along the edge of the river where the snook would be hiding, but I didn't recognize any of the spots. I was about to get discouraged when I made a perfect cast up under some mangrove limbs and got a nice blowup on the lure. A fat little snook come in the boat that looked like he might fit in that unused spot in my ice chest I had saved for a dinner trout.

With the dinner question well on its way to being resolved, I decided to head on up the river and see if I could find the old man's place again before it got dark, or I got lost.

Chapter 53

Sara

Sara stayed up late, listening to the boys talking about Disneyworld and the things they planned to do. They were such an amazing pair, she had no doubt they could do just about anything they wanted, whether it was in the wilderness or a big city. She slept soundly and didn't wake up until early afternoon.

There was no sign of the two boys; they obviously were gone. Sara felt sad about their leaving, and a little hurt that they hadn't said goodbye. They would be missed.

She started a fire in the little stove to heat water and took a sniff of the contents of several jars from the shelf that the boys had said were tea. She decided on one that had a minty aroma and looked through the pile of paperback books while she waited for the water to boil. Down toward the bottom of the pile was a worn old copy of one of Charlie Spider's first books.

With the events of the last few days, she hadn't thought as much about Charlie. Seeing the old book brought it all back. With her new friends gone, the feelings of loneliness were stronger than ever. She wished she had asked Newt about bringing Charlie back once she had all three of the Chacmools. Of course it was a moot point, since she was no closer to having the third idol than she had been when she left California. The boys had been very vague about where it was. Anytime she tried to ask them about the missing idol, they had just told her to stay at the cabin and be patient.

* * *

Her skiff was still where they had hidden it, back up under some dense mangroves, safe from the curious eyes of Park helicopters. The little dugout canoe was still there as well. Sara decided there must have been another the boys had used to go meet their friend Horse.

She hadn't tried the little craft by herself before, but it looked easy enough. The balance thing was a little tricky, standing up and poling, but before long she had the narrow little canoe moving along through the swamp like she had been doing it all her life.

Feeling quite pleased with herself, Sara decided to head over to the garden to pick up some vegetables for soup and some firewood for the stove. It was then that she saw a flats boat with a tall thin man poling along. He was headed right toward her and the cabin.

Chapter 54

Taco Bob Returns to the Cabin

"Soup is good food!"

I was getting a little worried that maybe I'd passed the cabin or taken a wrong turn somewhere. I had fresh batteries in my GPS and some spares to boot since my little experience with the fog in Cedar Key. The GPS said I was close when I seen the old man up ahead a ways standing in his canoe. I was sure glad to see the little fella, and gave him a yell and a wave.

As I poled up through the shallow water in between the mangroves, I noticed something wasn't quite right. Mr. Small had gone still as soon as I called out and hadn't moved a twitch as I came up closer. His clothes didn't look right either, and he might have even grown an inch or two. It looked like Mr. Small's boat though, and I could just make out the outline of the cabin back in the mangroves, but that wasn't the old man in the dugout.

"Howdy! Looking for Mr. Small. He around?"

It was kinda hard to tell with the big floppy hat, but it was starting to look like a young woman. A rather nervous young woman.

"Name's Taco Bob. I'm kind of a friend of Mr. Small's."

"He's not here."

"Okay. You expecting him back soon? I kind of went out of my way a bit here to come by and see him."

I'd stopped poling about ten feet away. The woman in Mr. Small's boat didn't seem real talkative.

"You a friend of his, young lady?"

The hat tilted back a bit and the woman gave me a defiant look.

"I am Sara! I have come to find the Golden Chacmool Idol!"

This was something. A good conversation starter at least.

"Uh, is it a little statue about the size of your hand? Got the head of a woman and the body of an animal?"

I had her attention with that. Thought she might be talking about the little gold good-luck charm Mr. Small had been using for a doorstop before he gave it to me.

"Yes, it was part of a treasure at one time. Do you have it?"

I kinda patted my pockets like I was looking for it. I gave her a smile and a wink.

"As a matter of fact I do have a little statue like that, but I don't seem to have it on my person right at the moment."

This bit of news didn't seem to be playing too good, judging by the look on the young woman's face.

"I do, however, know where there's a statue like that though."

This was a little better received, and I might have even seen the first little bit of a smile.

"Is it in your boat? Do you have it with you?" She definitely was worked up over that little statue.

"No, I would imagine it's somewhere," I took a look at my watch, "between Homestead and Key Largo about now. But don't worry none; it's in good hands."

It was time to get on to more important things than gold doorstops.

"I really would like to know where Mr. Small is, young lady. Have you seen him?"

She looked down a second, then back at me.

"I don't know where Mr. Small is. I was told there was an old man who lived out here who used to look for pirate treasure, I guess that would be your Mr. Small. Mr. Willie didn't remember —"

"Mr. Willie? You know Mr. Willie from Key West?"

This was some news for me, and the woman calling herself Sara was picking up on it there too.

"Yes! Two Willies helped me learn about the boat so I could come here! They are my dear friends."

Now we were getting somewhere, though I wasn't too sure how this little woman would know those two fellas.

"Well, they're purty good friends of mine too. Looks like we might have something in common here."

We were both smiling now.

"Suppose we start working toward continuing this conversation inside before it gets dark and we're standing out here feeding the skeeters?"

"Yes, they'll be bad soon. Do you like soup? I was just about to go get some vegetables for soup."

This sounded good, and strangely familiar. I stepped back and opened the icebox and held up the snook I had in there.

"I kind of had my heart set on fish soup, if you don't mind."

Her eyes got big looking at that fish and she came up with a full-scale grin at last.

* * *

Between the two of us, we seemed to pretty well know our way around the cabin and finally got some soup cooking on the stove that evening. While we were sitting there at the table waiting, a thunderstorm rumbled out over the Gulf and a fresh breeze found its way through the window screen. We both asked about the things we were most concerned with. Sara kept asking about the little statue, and I was still curious about Mr. Small. I was also wondering about her being out there by herself.

The little statues Sara showed me looked almost exactly like the one I had, all right. After I had her convinced that the other statue was fine in my old truck and safely on its way down to Key West, I asked her what she wanted it for anyway. I told her I wasn't all that excited about giving it up, since Mr. Small had given it to me as a souvenir and all. She said she only wanted to borrow it. What she wanted it for wouldn't take long. It was kind of an experiment, and she swore I would get it back unharmed. I told her I didn't see any reason why I couldn't loan it to her sometime when we got back to Key West. Figured I'd be asking Mr. Willie what he knew about this strange girl first though.

Sara got all happy when I told her I'd loan her the statue and proceeded to tell me all about the young boy who had been at the cabin. She seemed to be really taken with the whole wilderness thing and was going on about how Henry had shown her such wondrous things out in the swamp.

"You say this boy's name was Henry? Did he mention Mr. Small? Was he some sort of kin to him?"

Sara looked down a bit.

"I really didn't find out much about the old man who used to live here. They just said that there used to be an old man here who had been a treasure hunter."

It was sounding like the old man was really gone. My disappointment must have shown.

"I'm sorry your friend is gone. I wish I had asked more about him when Henry was here."

"Sara, you said 'they' a minute ago. Was there someone else here besides the boy Henry?"

She hesitated just a second.

"No." She jumped up and went to the stove. "Just Henry. I think this is about done. Want to have a look?"

I decided to let it go and have some soup.

* * *

While we ate us some extra fine fish soup, we compared stories on hanging out in the swamp — her with the boy Henry and me with old Mr. Small. There were a lot of similarities in our stories, and I was getting really curious about this young fella.

We polished off that whole pot of soup between us and got things cleaned up and put away. I realized there was a problem with the sleeping arrangements when we both headed for the mat at the far side of the room. That mat had given me some of the best night's sleep of my life, and I was determined to sleep there.

Sara obviously felt the same way because she sat on it the same time I did. We kind of laughed a little, and I told her there was a blanket in my boat that she was welcome to use. She told me there was a brand new sleeping bag in her skiff that I could try out.

When neither one of us made any kind of move to get up, Sara scooted back off the pad and gently pushed me so I would lay down. It was looking like she was going to give me the pad, so I took off my shoes and lay on my side curled up a little with my back to the wall. She watched me until I was comfortable, then wiggled in with me on the pad spoon-style with her butt and back firmly against me. I didn't think this was going to work at all, and then she started making purring noises and wiggling her butt against me.

It was dark in the cabin, but I could see she had a pretty big frown going when I pushed her off the pad and got up. I went outside and got the blanket and used it as a divider between us and told her it was back to back or she was sleeping on the floor. She looked like she was about to cry so I explained that it wasn't anything to do with her, that she was a very attractive young woman and a nice person, but there was someone I was seeing that I felt very strongly about.

None of this played too good to the home crowd, and I was feeling pretty lousy about things myself when I finally drifted off to sleep.

* * *

Trout soup

One nice trout (or snook) fillet
Couple medium white or sweet potatoes
One onion
Two or three carrots
Medium-size tomato if you've got one

A piece of gnarly brown root from the ceiling of a little cabin in the swamp (might substitute a little dried or fresh ginger)
Three heaping tablespoons of powder from the big gray jar on the shelf (maybe use flour or cornstarch instead)
Spoonful of powder from the coffee can on the top shelf (or some Cajun/Creole spice)

Cut everything up in small pieces. Get a couple of cups of water boiling, and cook taters and carrots a little. Cut the heat back and add the rest of the vegetables and fish. Stir in the spices and flour and simmer for an hour or so. Add water as needed.

If you want to get fancy, it's even better served with a little fresh heart of palm sliced thin and sprinkled on top.

Chapter 55
Taco Bob and His Spot

"A real nice surprise!"

I woke up for just a minute when Sara got up and went outside into the gray dawn. I was back sound asleep when she started yelling and calling my name. I came awake and grabbed my shoes, figuring she must have got herself snake bit or something. I was stumbling for the door when Sara burst in and we ran smack into one another. She was carrying something heavy that hit me in the chest and knocked the wind out of me and set me on my rear.

"Taco Bob! Look what I found! It was in my skiff!"

I was trying to get my breath while a very excited young woman dumped a cloth bag out in my lap. It was gold.

"It was in the console locker of the boat!"

I was still holding my chest with one hand and picking up gold necklaces and coins with the other. There was a big gold bowl in there too, must have been what got me so good.

"There's a note! Listen to this!" She held a paper in her hand. "For you, Sara, to help you with your journey."

She grabbed a necklace with big heavy links of gold and put it over her head, then scooped up coins and more necklaces with both hands. She was grinning and sitting there in front of me making happy sounds and kind of bouncing. Nothing like a bag of gold to make a girl happy.

"Wait! There's more writing on the back!" She dropped the gold and picked the note off the floor.

"If you have a guest, tell him to check his spot before he leaves." She stuck the paper in my face.

"Let's go look in your spot and see what's there!"

Sara was putting all the necklaces on and then putting everything else back in the bag while I read the note. The suddenly well-to-do young lady stood up and dumped the bag on the table so she could look through her loot more carefully.

"I can't believe this! It's like a dream!"

I was still in shock myself and didn't catch the significance at first of her staring at her hand right after she said that. She let out a little yip and went back to examining her gold. I finally got myself shook out and sat there at the table too.

"Sara, I got no idea where my spot is, or even if I'm the guest the note is talking about."

She didn't take her eyes off the coin she was holding up to the light.

"Think about it some. Maybe it's that sleeping pad you're so fond of." I got a hard glance and a quick frown. She slapped the coin down on the table. "I bet it's buried somewhere! Maybe in the garden! Did you have a favorite spot in the garden when you were here before?"

I was thinking about it, but before I could say anything, Sara had her gold back in the bag again and announced we were going to the garden.

* * *

Acting like she was Cleopatra, Queen of the Nile, Sara sat in the front of the little canoe while I stood in back and poled. She'd put on a few rings and was admiring them as we moved through the water toward the garden. She was still wearing the necklaces and had the bag in her lap.

"I never really had any money of my own before. I don't even know what I should buy. Maybe a new car? Maybe a shiny new sports car!"

"You might as well. Seems like they're everywhere you look these days."

"And a house? Maybe my own boat too, and some nice clothes!"

"I would imagine the gold you got there would be worth enough you could get yourself just about anything you want. You just got to decide what it is you really want."

She turned around and stared at me. It was like a shadow crossed over her face. She turned back around facing the front of the canoe and got all serious.

"I know what I want. I know exactly what I want. Let's see if we can find your spot, then we can go back to Key West."

Since it looked like the chances of finding Mr. Small were slim to none, that was sounding like the right plan to me.

* * *

The garden was looking good; somebody'd been taking care of it since I'd seen it last. I walked around a little, and

Sara just sat down in the shade of a big oak still wearing her gold and swatted a few bugs.

I could maybe understand the boy leaving some gold for Sara in her skiff before he left. He must have come up on a big treasure haul that Mr. Small had somewhere. Might explain why the old fella had been using a little gold statue for a doorstop. I wasn't sure why this boy I'd never met would be leaving anything for me though, that is, if I was the guest the note was talking about.

I'd checked out the sleeping pad back at the cabin real good before we left. Nothing there, and I couldn't recall any kind of place that might be my "spot" out there at the garden. I found the old rusty garden shovel and went poking around an area where the old man and I had been sitting and talking one time. Tried digging a little around where I had helped plant some tomatoes once but only found some worms and a sleepy little toad. I looked over to where Sara had been watching my every move, but she must have had to go off into the bushes. I decided to take a quick one myself and was careful to avoid the patch of poison ivy the old man had showed me once. I got over to a place in the palmetto shrubs where I knew there wasn't any ivy and had one of my rare brainstorms. It didn't seem too likely, but that was a spot I had used a few times before. I went back and got the shovel and dug up a cloth sack of gold right where I had been about to go.

I made Sara pole back to the cabin, since I was too excited and busy inspecting my own little pile of treasure. It was more coins and gold chains, some medallions and even a gold dagger with some kind of jewels set in the handle. There was some mighty impressive stuff, and I was a bit stunned by it all.

"I can be ready to leave for Key West as soon as we get back to the cabin."

Sara's voice kind of brought me back a little. She had taken off her gold jewelry and was all business.

"I reckon we can head on over. It looks like a good day, and the wind ain't bad yet."

I tried asking her about how the boy Henry would know to bury that gold in that spot and was she sure he hadn't said anything about Mr. Small. She seemed to have her mind on other things and didn't to want to talk much, so I let it go, figuring I'd try asking her again in Key West.

We got things stowed away at the cabin and set off in our boats poling through the swamp toward the river. If we didn't run into any problems, I figured we could make KW before dark easy. Sara was poling her boat behind mine and I was concentrating on getting out of there without getting lost.

"Hey, Taco Bob, I just thought of something! When I was in Key West, the place was crazy with people getting ready for some kind of big show. I sure hope that's over by now and everything is back to normal."

Chapter 56

Key West

With the big concert coming that evening, US 1 into Key West was even more jammed than ever. The bumper-to-bumper traffic was at a crawl and backed up almost to Miami by mid-day. For every vehicle leaving Key West, there were twenty trying to get in.

Food, souvenir t-shirts, sunscreen, beer, and other emergency supplies had been airlifted into the Navy base and distributed on an as-needed basis to the bars, restaurants, and shops of Key West. Most of the streets were filled with parked RVs, vans, and cars that had become temporary shelter for their owners. Even with so many of the streets blocked, the bikers were still able to cruise around easily. The whole island rumbled with the sound of motorcycles.

The police had given up on arresting people for public nudity and intoxication since the latest Fantasy Fest parade the night before and were concentrating on working the larger beer and food riots with the National Guard.

The water around the island continued to fill with boats. Hundreds of boats. Every type of water vessel imaginable, from giant cruise ships to canoes, and even a few Cuban refugees in large inner tubes who'd made the trip for the show. The turquoise sea surrounding Key West was looking like a huge marina.

The USNS Mercy hospital ship had been brought in the day before and was doing a brisk business treating tourists and boaters for exposure, alcohol overdoses, gunshot wounds, boating accidents, and shark bites.

Besides the Navy helicopters ferrying people back and forth to the hospital ship, there were police helicopters, National Guard helicopters, Coast Guard helicopters, and numerous media helicopters buzzing around overhead. In addition, the sky was filled with small sightseeing planes, planes pulling advertising banners, Navy cargo planes, commercial air traffic into Key West International, as well as several blimps, including one shaped like an opossum.

Chapter 57

Getting Ready

Carol was pissed. Jeremy had come back from paying off the fortuneteller with the news.

It seems the spirits hadn't given her any clues as to the whereabouts of Sara, but they had indicated to Mama Rosa that there was a mysterious man looking for the Chacmools. A large man with a shaved head was the key to the idols, a man named Saul Thorpe.

Jeremy couldn't understand why Carol wasn't happy until she told him Thorpe was the name of the guy the agency in LA had hired to find the idols for her. Carol was pissed.

* * *

Saul Thorpe figured he needed a gun. Found out from one of the neighbors in Orlando the reason no one seemed to be around the apartment was they'd all gone to Key West. Told some geek neighbor he was a fishing buddy of the guy with the truck and boat. Was supposed to hook up for some fishing. Geek was a fisherman, ready to tell all he knew. All he knew was they went to Key West.

Hand was still a little swollen, threw off his aim for gumming. That really sucked. Traffic got real bad into the Keys. All these people weren't going to help either. Make it harder to find the guy. Maybe find the woman and dog though, a start.

Still hurting from the dog bites. Hurt to sit down even. Fucking dog was one reason he needed a gun.

* * *

Marty the Manatee was ready. He'd been getting ready for coming out of retirement for years. While he was enjoying life as a recluse on his island in the Caribbean, the media rumor mill kept his image alive.

"Marty thought to be talking to Russians about going up as space tourist."

"Marty seen in England talking to Queen."

"Marty busted in Daytona Beach strip club dressed as Pee Wee Herman."

The end result of the media attention was ever-increasing record sales and Marty's popularity approaching that of living legend.

The band had moved to the island a couple of years earlier. They practiced twice a week, and Marty could belt out a song better than ever. He ran on the beach everyday, worked out, and lived on salads, fruit, and seafood. He had lost most of the excess weight and had a special body suit made up to make him look fat for when he made his return to the stage. The offer from the Governor of Florida to play in Key West was just the opportunity he had been waiting for. Marty was very ready.

* * *

Governor Walker was nervous. The whole Key West thing was supposed to draw attention away from the now-famous Southernmost Bandit, and it had done that. But the advertising blitz for the event had worked so well, it was causing a situation in Key West that might eventually require declaring martial law.

The plan was for the Governor to be on stage to introduce Marty and the opening act. Since the event was being carried live by at least three networks, it was an excellent chance for some spontaneous politicking. The Governor's speechwriters had put together a magnificent piece of work that would rival Martin Luther King Jr. or John F. Kennedy.

If they could only keep the lid on the situation in Key West caused by the crush of humanity that had shown up for the concert, it could be a big boost for the upcoming re-election campaign. Or if things went bad it could make him look like an incompetent boob. The Governor read over the speech again, but he was so nervous he couldn't concentrate.

* * *

Richard "Little Dick" Jawaski was dead. His biker brothers of the Key Biscayne Chapter of the Hog Fuckers Motorcycle Club had laid him to rest two days after the Coast Guard pulled his body from the water near the Seven Mile Bridge. Little Dick's old lady had been following him across the bridge in their station wagon and had fallen behind because she was changing a diaper on the youngest while she drove. She saw a van with a big bald man laughing hysterically coming in the other direction just before she saw the wrecked bike on the bridge.

Mrs. Jawaski taught computer language at a community college in Miami to supplement her husband's salary as a laboratory test case. She had a photographic memory and, even in her confusion and grief, had remembered the license tag number of the van.

The club had contacts in law enforcement, so running the tag and getting intel on the driver of the van was easy. After the funeral they handed out pictures and a description of the man they believed to be responsible for numerous motorcycle accidents that involved projectiles thrown from passing vehicles.

The other bike clubs agreed: They wanted to take care of this in-house and didn't want to get the police involved. Some of the accidents, like Little Dick's, had been fatal.

Chapter 58

Saul

Four hours in the hot sun to move twenty miles. Van was about to overheat. Only a couple miles from Key West now. Traffic was stopped because a truck full of portable toilets broke down up ahead.

Couple of ugly biker-types walking down the two lanes of stopped traffic looking in vehicles. Saw the one in the next lane was holding a picture up and looking in windows. Picture was of Saul. This was most likely a bad thing.

Traffic was starting to move up ahead, but the biker checking his lane was coming up to the van.

Had the big shades on already, put on a hat. Reach back around for the toolbox. Dirtbag comes to the window. Roll the window down and lean back so he has to get close to see in. Scooter trash was giving him the eye.

"How 'bout you lose the shades for me, baldy?"

Typical biker, greasy beard. Reach out and get a handful of chin hair, pull down and in. Reach quick with the other hand and linesman's pliers, grab a good hunk of tongue, and pull him close. Guy forgets about the shades, starts making funny noises. Sure enough, reach out the window and down — find a gun stuck under biker's shirt. Traffic moving.

Quick head butt and guy wants to lie down all of a sudden. Give him a little shove and catch up with traffic.

Chapter 59

Film at Eleven

A TV news crew was set up near the huge stage at the former site of the Southernmost Monument. Hundreds of people were wandering around the area already, several of whom bore a striking resemblance to Papa Hemingway.

A well-dressed young woman stood in front of the camera holding a microphone. An assistant was dabbing at the shoulder of her blazer with a damp towel. She did not look happy.

"I can't believe that fucking bird did that!"

The video crew was watching. The young woman gave them each a hard look. The members of the crew all seemed to be holding their breath. Someone snickered.

"I heard that!"

She shooed the assistant away and gave her clothes a quick check.

"Okay, let's try it again. Is the hair right?" The cameraman still seemed to be having trouble with speech. He just nodded and gave her a signal to continue.

"That's right, Peter. In just a short time the final parade of the Special Edition Southernmost Monument Benefit Key West Fantasy Fest will wind up right here where I'm standing. The Governor of Florida ..."

A fat, balding, middle-aged man, wearing only a Marty the Manatee t-shirt and holding a beer, staggered through the shot behind the reporter.

"... himself is expected to MC the benefit concert following the parade, featuring ..."

The man suddenly came back into the shot and looked toward the camera. He smiled a big drunken smile and waved.

"... the long-awaited return of the legendary singer/songwriter Marty the Manatee. As you know, Peter, these last few days have been quite chaotic here in Key West, as thousands of people ..."

The man mouthed, "Hi mom," then seemed to become aware of the young woman between himself and the camera.

"... have flocked to this small island to show their support for the efforts to raise money for a new monument after the Southernmost Bandit's daring ..."

The man killed the beer in one pull and belched. He looked down at his exposed lower body and then at the reporter standing in front of him. He smiled a wicked smile, closed his eyes, and started making a grinding motion with his pelvic area.

"...theft recently of the original. Now what's wrong with you morons?"

Chapter 60

Taco Bob Goes Home to Key West

"You never know who you're going to meet!"

Coming across Florida Bay toward Key West in the boats, the first thing Sara and I could see was the blimps. As we got a little closer, we could make out some small planes with long tails and dozens of helicopters buzzing around like a swarm of hornets.

About a mile from the island, we started to come up on the boats. Boats everywhere. Lots of boats had diver-down flags, and we saw people in the water holding up lobsters. There were folks fishing and water-skiing, and fast little jet-skis zipping around everywhere. Way more cruise ships than you'd ever want to see were anchored close in, with boats ferrying tourists to and from the island. There were sailboats, houseboats, cabin cruisers, kayaks, inflatable rafts, and a huge white boat with red crosses.

We slowed down and managed to work our way into the marina without getting run over. I was afraid we'd have a hard time finding a place to tie up, but it seemed just about everything that could float was either over on the south side of the island for the concert or heading out that way.

I got with Sara and told her that under the circumstances, we might want to wait until the next day to get back together so I could loan her the little Chacmool statue. She didn't like that idea at all, so I finally agreed to meet over at Mr. Willie's place after I'd found my truck and got the statue for her. Sara told me to go ahead while she got things squared away at the marina office.

Key West was a mess. A big Fantasy Fest parade was just starting when we got there, and people were heading that way on foot since most of the roads were blocked. Mary Ann was supposed to park my old truck at Pete's sister's place, which was on the exact other side of where the parade was happening. I could hear motorcycles roaring and marching bands starting up along the parade route a few blocks away. The road was barricaded off by the marina, so I took a convenient shortcut down an alley between two old warehouses. The buildings blocked the parade noise enough that I could plainly hear a sharp metallic click off to my left, kind of like the sound you'd expect jacking a cartridge into a large-caliber gun would make. I froze, then turned slowly, knowing all too well what I was likely to see. But I held out hope.

"Surprise! Did you miss us?"

So much for hope. Two big grins proudly showing off years of poor dental hygiene and what looked to be a fifty-caliber machine gun on a tripod, all aimed my way. Daltons.

"Got ya this time, Taco Bob! If you'd be so kind as to get those hands up, I'm kind of a stickler for tradition when it comes to killing folks in cold blood."

"Evening, George, Lenny. I see you haven't lost your sense of fair play either."

George, the small-statured mastermind of the two-man gang, gave the big gun a loving pat.

"Found this here beauty over at the Navy base. Them years of experience breaking into places comes in handy sometimes. I was hoping for depleted uranium bullets, but we had to settle for regular ammo. Hope you don't mind."

Big as a house and almost as talkative, Lenny held up an impressive cartridge belt that came out the side of the machine gun and went to a box on the ground.

"No, those'll be fine I'm sure. You boys got this planned out well. Timing's pretty impressive too."

"Hey, we're no small shakes at escaping from prison these days neither, long as we're giving credit where due."

George pulled out a cell phone and punched a number.

"I don't mean to be rude, but I gotta make one quick call, then we can get back to killing ya."

"Take your time, George. No hurry."

I tried to assess my current predicament. Another small alley behind the Daltons, next to an overflowing dumpster. Not much chance of making a run for it, not with George looking anxious behind the big gun. Hundreds of thousands of people crawling over Key West, and I was down the only deserted alley on the island.

"We got him!" George put the phone away and went back to grinning like a possum.

"Something going on here I should know about, George? You boys working for somebody? Wouldn't be a big guy with a shaved head, would it?"

Instead of answering, the Daltons looked at each other and busted out laughing.

"I reckon you're going to find out soon enough!" George looked like he was dying to tell the story. Man always did appreciate a captive audience. "Funny how things work out. A few days ago, me and Lenny here were just hanging out, planning another of our ingenious escapes from prison. The DEA comes along, starts burning a few hundred bales of pot in the field next-door from a big drug bust. Maybe it was just the thunderstorm coming in, maybe it was them hundreds of prisoners praying hard, but the wind changed direction just right.

"So while all the cons and guards were facing into the wind hyperventilating, we took the warden's car for a quick test drive. Piece of shit by the way. Those Lexus cars are way overrated. They drift on corners and don't float in canals. I'm a Chevy man, myself."

I heard a vehicle going down the street. Without turning my head, I could see a camo-colored truck go by out of the corner of my eye.

"Anyway, after water testing the car, Lenny cleaned out a buffet table in Homestead."

This got Lenny grinning and rubbing his belly appreciatively.

"Walked out of the restaurant onto the street and held up a sign 'DIRTY DEEDS DONE CHEAP.' Hour later we had us a ride to Key West and the perfect job."

George pulled out a big wad of cash.

"Yep, job of a lifetime. All we had to do was block off the street by the marina and wait here in the alley for the airplane pilot to call, then keep a guy around till the boss showed. Imagine my surprise when we found out the guy's name was Taco Bob."

George winked big and shoved the money back in his pants pocket.

"Boss didn't say what was going to happen to you, but I'm in such a good mood today, I'm seriously considering throwing in killing ya at no extra charge."

He gave the gun a loving pat.

"I figure a few hundred rounds with ol' Betsy here ought to do the job!"

George got busy with a round of insane laughter and didn't notice a black Harley coming down the alley behind him until his partner tapped him on the shoulder.

"Alright, this should be the boss." George looked back at me and gave me his best evil grin, "Won't be long now, Taco Bob!"

The bike stopped a good twenty feet behind the Daltons. Saul Thorpe didn't look that big to me, sitting on the Harley. The black helmet and tinted face shield came off, and there was a good-looking woman instead. She parked the bike, walked up next to Lenny, and stood there with her arms crossed. I couldn't place her right off, maybe it was the black leather jacket and pants, but she did look awful familiar. She also looked mighty pissed.

"Where is Ponce?"

Which would explain the familiar. She was the latest girlfriend I had seen Ponce with.

"And don't lie to me. I've been following you by land, sea, and air for days. I know you must have met with him."

Which would likely explain the increase in sports cars and air traffic I'd seen lately. Before I could say anything, she tossed her long dark hair back and gave me a good solid glare.

"I almost missed you when I got the call from Ponce's landlady. Luckily that funky truck of yours is easy to spot, even doing ninety down US 1."

The red Corvette.

"An associate hired these men to wait for you here," she looked around Lenny and took a half-step back, obviously noticing the machine gun and wild-eyed George for the first time, "while I used my father's assets to follow you."

She could tell I didn't know what she was talking about and came up with a smug smile, "My father is Crazy Roy. Perhaps you've heard of him?"

Who hadn't? Owner of Crazy Roy's Big Boys Toys? based in Miami and featuring every kind of non-essential, high-dollar "toy" every red-blooded man in the country was dying to have.

I noticed a cat over by the dumpster behind the Daltons.

"Young lady, I know this ain't exactly what you're wanting to hear, but I haven't seen Ponce, and I got no idea where he is."

I was right, she definitely didn't want to hear that, at all.

"Ha! Liar! He told me he was going to the swamp to look for his silly Fountain of Youth, and our planes followed you to the biggest swamp in the world — the Everglades!" She looked over at George, still pointing the big gun my way. "Does that thing work?"

"You kidding? Want I should shoot off an arm? Maybe a leg?"

I saw a man walk by at the far end of the alley.

"Maybe you could just shoot by his feet, like they do in those old Westerns?" I could tell her heart wasn't in anybody getting hurt.

"Like this?"

The gun made a helluva noise and bullets kicked up the dust by my feet. I did a little involuntary dance step. The short burst of machine-gun fire had George jumping up and down.

"Hot damn! That was fun! Don't spill the beans too quick, Taco Bob. I got plenty of ammunition!"

Lenny grinned and held up the ammo belt. As the dust settled, the man I'd seen was coming down the alley. He wasn't a big man, and kinda thin. As he got closer I could see he had a pointy goatee beard and was carrying a cat. Ponce.

"Taco Bob!"

He walked past the others without giving them a glance and set the cat down by my feet.

"Que pasa, mi amigo!"

Ponce gave me a big smile and a bigger hug, all back slapping and happy.

"I am so glad to see you, Senor Taco!"

Man was about to hug the stuffing out of me. I stood there with my hands up in the air still, not sure what to do.

"I'm proud to see you too, Ponce. You happened along at just the right time, I'd say."

He turned loose and stood there grinning at me.

"I am just back in Key West today! I went to the house of the Two Willies. They say Mary Ann has your truck and to check around the marina. So I am on my way to the marina, I hear a loud noise, and here you are!"

This was followed by another rib-cracking hug. Ponce finally broke and spun around, looking at the Daltons.

"And these? These must be the famous Dalton Gang! So nice to meet you! I've heard much about you!"

He gave each Dalton a hearty handshake, then turned slowly and menacingly toward the woman.

"Angelina! Why are you here!"

She gave Ponce a look cold enough to freeze spit.

"I am looking for you, believe it or not!"

Ponce was giving her the look right back.

"Ha! For what then? To make fun of my inherent quest for everlasting youth? To tell me again I am not man enough for you because I juggle cats for a living?"

This last bit got Angelina. She lost the ice in her eyes and hung her head. Ponce stayed on it.

"This is what you told me, remember? That is why I left!"

Angelina didn't look up, mumbling something. Ponce stood his ground, defiant as ever.

"What are you saying, woman? I cannot hear you!"

"I said, I was wrong! Ever since you left, all I can think about is you. I followed your friend here across Florida hoping to find you."

Now Ponce was easing back.

"Really?"

"Yes, really."

Angelina was crying now.

"And because . . ."

Everyone stared at the attractive young woman in black leather. She looked Ponce dead in the eye.

"And because, I'm pregnant!"

Ponce stepped back, like he'd taken a punch to the forehead, then rushed to Angelina.

"A baby! An heir! Oh, Angelina!"

While the happy parents-to-be were holding each other and bawling like babies themselves, I still had my hands up and George was rolling his eyes. The happy couple grabbed the cat and waved a tearful farewell, roaring off on the big motorcycle. Which left me with my hands up in front of the

Dalton Gang and a large machine gun. I decided to try something.

"Lenny, bet they got some mighty fine eats over at the parade. Conch fritters, grouper sandwiches, lobster casserole."

Lenny was drooling, George was angry.

"You hush now, Taco Bob! Don't be trying none of your tricks on Lenny here."

It looked like I was about to get another dancing lesson, so I decided to let it slide. There was a noise between the buildings then, followed by a most lovely sight — a National Guard tank with a loudspeaker.

"You, with the machine gun. Step away from the machine gun. NOW!"

George and Lenny, not fully grasping the situation, turned their gun toward the tank. I decided this was an excellent time for me to continue on my journey to check on my truck. I ran as fast as my legs would take me, but looked back when a warning shot from the tank hit the dumpster behind the Daltons. The last I saw, they were holding their hands up and looking a bit dazed.

* * *

I managed to get through the mass of humanity whooping it up with the parade going on in Old Town. It was kind of like the Possum Gras parades I remembered from my Texas days, except for all the painted naked people, riots, and National Guard troops. Most of the side streets were full of all kinds of cars, trucks, and RVs where folks were camping out and living in their vehicles. There wasn't all that many people around though, because everybody was either at the parade or heading over to the concert place.

I was happy to find my old truck there at One-Eyed Pete's sister's place, parked in the side yard like before. It looked like Mary Ann had been sleeping in my little homemade camper on the back all right. I dug around under the mattress and found the little statue. It was going to be a mite cramped with the two of us trying to sleep on that small of a bed. But I figured that would be a good problem to have.

Nobody was home at the house and my bicycle wasn't in the back yard, so I figured Mary Ann was using it like I'd told her. I hoofed it back across the island and got to Mr. Willie's place just before dark. Sara was there with the two Willie's, all teary-eyed and handing out hugs to everyone after I gave her the little gold statue. She said she'd bring it back later on, and then she took off into the night.

Chapter 61

Jeremy

Jeremy figured Carol must be starting her period or something, since she was being even more of a hard-nosed bitch than usual. Instead of thanking him for getting that information from the fortuneteller, she had gotten all mad. Women.

Carol had ordered him to get out on the streets and find Sara and not come back without her stupid Chacmools. Yeah, right. Jeremy had found some money in Carol's bag when she went to the can back in her hotel room, so it was time to party.

The parade was going on with all those hot-looking, drunk women everywhere wearing long strings of beads and not much else. Someone ordering emergency supplies to be flown into Key West must have mixed up the order for bottled water and tequila. The result was a drinking water shortage, and premium tequila was going for a dollar a bottle on Duval Street. If it wasn't for Carol, Jeremy figured he'd be having the time of his life.

As he headed for the parade, Jeremy thought he saw someone who looked like Sara coming from the marina. It was hard to tell because she was so damn ordinary looking. Jeremy was torn for a moment, but decided to follow her when a jolt from the collar around his neck reminded him of Carol. She must have discovered she was light some cash.

By the time he could see straight again, and he'd made sure the jolt hadn't caused him to bite off his tongue, Sara was gone. Jeremy panicked and ran off in the direction she'd been going. He caught sight of her going into a little house. He still wasn't sure it was her but figured it was worth hanging around for a few minutes.

Chapter 62

Saul

Saul finally got into Key West. The roads were jammed, so he had to drive through a few yards and down some sidewalks. Parked the van over by the house where the fisherman Taco Bob had been leaving his truck. Familiar-looking truck with a funky camper and boat trailer parked there this time. Time to put on the wig and mustache he had in his bag. Stupid bikers.

About to go take a look in the camper when a tall thin guy walks up and unlocks the door and goes inside. Even better. Slip up for a little chat.

Guy comes right back out and is around the back of the house and down the street. Gotta move quick, guy is a fast walker. Guy walks across the island and goes into a little house just before dark. More waiting. Stake out the house, sitting on a parked car. A few streetlights to cut the darkness. Try out the new look with the wig, wave to the bikers going down the street. Dirt bags wave back.

Little guy across the street sitting on the curb seems to be watching the house too.

Chapter 63

Jeremy

Jeremy wanted to party. He'd been sitting outside the house in the dark waiting for some woman that might not even be Sara for too long. Some tall guy had gone in there, but nobody had come out. He had to be careful; he remembered Sara had a lot of martial arts training.

There was music in the distance and only a few stragglers on the streets; almost everyone was at the concert. Jeremy was working up a real good case of self pity when somebody came out of the house and headed straight for him. He crouched down behind a car and waited. The person coming looked like her, all right. Jeremy stood up.

"Sara?"

Chapter 64

Saul

Saul winced when the little guy hit the woman in the forehead with a board. He could hear the crack the blow made from where he sat. Woman went down like a sack of potatoes.

Little guy fumbled around there in the dark and came up with a bag, looked inside, and took off running. What to do. Went over to check out the woman. Little mousy thing, not much. Looked a little like the picture the agency sent. Wasn't out, but definitely down for the count.

Decided to run down the little guy and see what he had. Might just be a purse, might be a little gold idol. Only one way to find out.

Little guy was hauling and got to a hotel before Saul could make the intercept.

Chapter 65

Jeremy

"Open the fucking door, Carol!"

Jeremy was pounding on the door to Carol's room and sweating buckets. He thought he was going to have a heart attack or something. He had trouble getting his breath, since he hadn't run farther than to the bathroom in years.

* * *

Carol was spread out on the bed watching the concert on TV. There were some good close-up shots of the lead singer of the opening band — he still had a nice body for his age. Jeremy's pounding on the door was becoming a bit distracting. She reached into her bag for the transmitter.

"I told you not to come back here without my property! Now go away!"

Jeremy finally got in a couple of good breaths.

"I got the Chacmools! Now open the…"

Carol had Jeremy by the dog collar and was dragging him in the door before he could finish. She grabbed the bag out of his hands and ripped it open.

She froze, then slowly took each of the three Chacmools out of the bag and gently laid them on the bed. There was a knock at the door, a male voice.

"Room service!"

Carol and Jeremy looked at each other.

"Did you order something?"

"No! I was going to order later!"

Carol looked worried, she turned toward the door.

"I didn't order anything!"

"Complimentary Margaritas, ma'am."

Before she could stop him, Jeremy opened the door. A tall, unhappy-looking Hispanic man handed Jeremy two Margaritas from a cart. Jeremy threw a dollar on the cart and slammed the door.

They killed the 'Ritas. The tossed glasses shattered against the wall. Carol gave Jeremy a big hug and looked about to cry from happiness.

There was another knock at the door.

"Who is it?"

"Land Shark."

Chapter 66

Saul

Saul finally caught up to the little guy. Guy was pounding on a door in the hotel, said "Chacmool," then disappeared inside. About to check it out when some spic guy comes by with a room service cart. Get scarce until the spic goes to the next floor.

Go to the door and get funny. Nobody laughing, no sense of humor. Hotel doors look stronger than they are. Couple shots with the biker's gun and the lock's gone and kick it in. Little guy and some hot broad are breaking huddle. Put the gun in some faces, everybody stays still. Hands up.

Three little gold idols on the bed. Jackpot! Pop guy in the head hard with the gun; he goes down. Broad gets hysterical, says Chacmools are leaving over her dead body. Tell her that won't really be necessary. Shoot her one time in the leg. Looks shocked like she can't believe it, then keels over. Down and out. Handy bag there on the bed; pick up the gold and split.

Chapter 67

Sara

Sara was on her feet, but still kind of shaky. Somebody had really let her have it with a piece of lumber. She remembered a familiar voice saying her name, then some big guy with stringy hair and a mustache. The bag with the Chacmools was gone. She had no idea what to do.

There was music in the air, coming from behind her. She turned and could see the glow in the night sky coming from the concert. The streets were deserted, no one around, just the usual cats and a stray dog or two.

Someone was moving, down toward the end of the street. A big guy walking fast past a streetlight took a left before she could get a good look. Sara shook herself out and ran through some backyards and got a look at the guy. He was holding her bag and heading for the other side of the island.

She ran along behind a row of parked cars until she was ahead of him, then came off the hood of a Volvo and caught the guy in the face with a good solid sidekick. Guy stood there holding his face while she did a roll on the ground. Sara came back up and gave him three uppercuts in the groin. That straightened up his legs for another solid side-kick, this one to the knee. The guy's leg made a sickly crack and he went down hard, screaming. She had to give him a few more kicks in the face before he let go of the bag. Somewhere in the struggle the guy's hair came off.

Sara started running, then heard a gunshot and something whiz by her head. She looked back and saw the guy still on the ground, but aiming a gun at her, ready to take another shot. Then two bikers were there; one kicked the gun away. Keep running.

The power place where she'd had the vision was where she needed to go to use the Chacmools, the place where they had been building the big stage.

Soon she would be with her beloved Charlie again.

Chapter 68

The Benefit Concert

Before the Fantasy Fest parade went down Duval Street to the concert site, the Hemingway Look-a-Like contest had been held on the giant stage. The stage was big enough to hold all the contestants and judges. It went to the edge of the water on the southernmost side. Coming from one side of the stage was a plywood ramp that went down to a cluster of trailers and support vehicles surrounded by a tall chain-link fence.

The rest of the land surrounding the stage was packed with people. By the time the sun was nearing the horizon, there were thousands of people ready for the sun to set and the show to begin. There wasn't much breeze, and it had been an especially hot afternoon, so National Guard troops had been distributing bottled water to the crowd for several hours. When they ran out of water they began handing out bottles of tequila. Food cannons onstage were blasting bags of snacks to the crowd. The main problem was the lack of sanitary facilities. There had been only two truckloads of portable toilets available on such short notice, and one of those was broken down somewhere along A1A.

The people on the water side of the stage didn't have that problem. Thousands more people were in boats or else just standing in the clear shallow water that stretched out for over a hundred yards from shore before it got deep. Luckily there was a strong tide, and the current was washing most of the waste and trash out to sea. Some of the closest boats had been anchored for days to get a good spot, and their occupants looked sunburned even in the dimming light.

As the sun came down to meet the ocean, the sky was clearing of air traffic and the high clouds on the horizon turned several shades of pink and crimson. It was a magnificent sunset and the huge crowd quieted in awe of nature's incredible display, until the only sound was the occasional bloodcurdling scream of someone in the water stepping on a stingray or sea urchin.

Every eye was to the west as the sun touched the water and began to slowly elongate like a candle flame. There was a hint of rumble from behind, and five Navy fighter jets came over the Southernmost Point at treetop level and screamed off into the sunset as the last of the candle flickered out. The noise of the jets shook the ground, and the crowd went apeshit. Everyone was cheering and applauding when the Governor of Florida ran onto the stage grinning and waving. The crowd continued to cheer as the Governor realized his microphone wasn't working and no one could hear what he was saying. The noise of the jets was replaced with a rumbling from the dozens of speakers set around the stage. The Governor threw down his speech and stomped off the stage.

The rumbling turned into the opening notes of a song as the warm-up band, a group of veteran British rockers who called themselves the Rolling Stones, ran onto the stage for a solid two hours of polished classics and lively new material.

After three encores, and a few minutes for the crowd to catch their breath after the incredible set that would be made into a movie and multi-platinum CD, the Governor came on stage again.

He was greeted with loud boos that turned to cheers when it became apparent that his mike still wasn't working. Another low rumble started as roadies cleared the stage and the Governor dejectedly walked down the ramp.

Chapter 69

Sara

Sara didn't have any trouble slipping past the security people and getting under the stage. The tremendous noise from the band stopped and was replaced by applause and cheering as they left the stage.

It was hard to concentrate, but Sara eventually managed to get her thoughts to quiet. She crawled around in the dark under the stage until she could feel she was in the right place. She took out the Chacmools.

Lying on her back with a Chacmool at each ear, she held the idol with its eyes open in her left hand, and the gold scarf from the bottom of the bag in her right. Simultaneously she set the Chacmool over her eyes and the scarf over her mouth. There was a low rumbling, and then she was no longer under the stage.

Chapter 70

Marty the Manatee

The rumble got louder and all the lights on the towers above the stage went off. After a few seconds, a single white spotlight shone on the ramp leading to the stage. This was what everyone had been waiting for — this was why they were there.

The rumbling had been coming from offstage, but now it was coming out of the speakers too. Just as the rumbling and suspense were becoming unbearable, a gold Harley came flying up the ramp with the single spotlight on it. The bike came to the end of the ramp and flew through the air for a good twenty feet before hitting the stage on its side. Just as it landed, hundreds of fireworks went off, lasers and strobes came from everywhere. The rider jumped off the bike the instant it hit the stage, and the big gray figure stood in the spotlight on the smoky stage with his arms above his head as the bike skidded into a stack of speakers and burst into flames. Pyrotechnics continued to explode overhead as the rest of the band rode up the ramp on Harleys and circled around Marty.

The next day, several people said that was when they saw a small, naked, gray-haired man standing in the smoke on the edge of the stage. The man smiled and held up his arms to the thousands of cheering people just as someone tackled him hard and dragged him off the stage.

The band parked their Harleys behind Marty as the smoke started to clear, and dozens of roadies ran out on the stage and set up equipment like they were doing an Indy Car pitstop. They put out the burning motorcycle and drove the bikes back down the ramp as the last of the fireworks stopped and all the lights went out again.

The crowd was wired but quieted down quickly. The single spot came back on the man dressed like a manatee standing center stage with his guitar. The crowd held its breath. Marty strummed his first cord of the night.

"Tired of the snow, but I know which way to go."

The crowd lost it. People fell out of boats, out of trees, and off rooftops. There was a collective sigh from the crowd that could be heard for miles.

* * *

Marty and his band played every one of his old songs at least twice. The crowd knew most of the words and sang along. They wouldn't let Marty leave, so he sang a few new songs after he made the crowd promise to let him go before dawn. He played his last song just as the first light of day could be seen in the eastern sky.

Chapter 71

Sara

Sara missed the concert. While thousands cheered and sang along, she slipped out unnoticed carrying an unconscious naked man over her shoulder. Poor Charlie hit his head when he went down on the stage and had been out since.

She trudged down the deserted streets to Mr. Willie's, where the bag of Chacmools went on the front porch for Taco Bob. Then she headed for the marina.

The boat was hers, paid for with a few of the gold treasure coins as soon as she'd come back to Key West. She'd had to give the man more than she suspected was fair, but he did throw in some extra tanks of gas. She wasn't worried though, she had plenty more gold hidden back at the garden up Lost Man's River.

She knew that was where they would go before she ever came back to Key West. No one to bother her or her lover out there. She was sure Charlie would learn to love the Everglades, and she would be there to take care of him always.

Chapter 72

Saul

Saul woke with a terrible headache. It was early morning and he was hurting. Riding in the back of a pickup with his back against the cab. Hands tied behind him.

Wasn't in the Keys anymore, must be up around the Everglades somewhere. He wasn't alone either. Sitting between two of the biggest bikers he had ever seen. The one sitting on his left poked him in a sore rib.

"Gum?"

Big piece of garbage was grinning and holding out a stick of gum. Didn't feel like gum, teeth didn't feel right.

Guy driving started banging on the back window. Two dirtbags stood up and pulled him to his feet. Showed him a concrete truck coming the other way. Big guys picked him up by the arms.

"Now!"

Chapter 73

Carol and Jeremy

When the police got to Carol's room, they thought Jeremy had shot her. Jeremy spent several hours in a makeshift cell at the high school before someone interviewed Carol at the hospital ship and decided he wasn't the perp.

The bullet was small caliber and made a clean wound in her thigh. Carol was released on crutches a couple of days later. After being questioned by the police about the dog collar on Jeremy and the transmitter they found in her bag, she booked a flight back to California, swearing she would never set foot in Florida again.

Jeremy was down to his last dollar by the time Carol got out of the hospital, so she told him to meet her at the airport. Then she took an earlier flight.

Chapter 74

Taco Bob's New Home

"Not sure about the yellow couch, though."

I got to see most of the concert from the roof of a friend of Mr. Willie's. Me and the two Willies stayed up there with his friend most of the night, enjoying the show.

We went dragging back over to Casa de Willie at dawn, all bleary-eyed but happy. I found my little statue and two more by the front door. No note or any sign of Sara

Three days later I was moving into my new place. A really nice old houseboat that the owner had just restored to its original condition. The fella had come up on a problem involving a gambling debt and was needing cash in a hurry. It took all the insurance money I'd been living on and the gold dagger with the jeweled handle, but the "Sandy-Bottomed Girl" was signed over to me along with the remaining nine and a half years of a ten-year lease on a choice boat slip in the marina.

Mary Ann and me had been staying at a motel in a little tiny room the last couple days while she was doing paperwork and having meetings with other security people and the police to get everything wrapped up. I'd showed her the gold treasure I'd come back from the Everglades with, then did the deal on the houseboat secret-like to surprise her.

She fell in love with the place just like I'd done, and I was proud to show it off to her before she went back to Orlando the next day. We sat around on the back deck of my new home, had a drink, and talked about treasure and musicians some more. I told her I figured that houseboat would be a good place to try my hand at writing about trout fishing in the weeks to come.

We'd heard that a Saul Thorpe had died in a bizarre head-on collision with a concrete truck a couple days earlier, so it didn't look like we were going to have to worry about him anymore. While Mary Ann was telling me more of what went on backstage at the concert, I was noticing a little shelf up in one corner that might be a nice place to set the little statues. I needed to dig 'em out and show 'em to Mary Ann sometime. She said the Sara I met there in the swamp sure sounded an awful lot like the one she knew from the Spider Cult.

Mary Ann finished her drink and announced that she was ready to try out the fancy bathroom on my new boat. After the big concert Mary Ann had got Marty to sign her chest with a black marker just before he got in his helicopter. Much to Mary Ann's chagrin, the autograph was wearing off, but we'd got a few interesting photos for the scrapbook she said she was going to start for my new coffee table.

In between going to historic concerts and closing deals on vintage houseboats, I'd managed to get in a little trout fishing around Key West. So while Mary Ann was getting cleaned up, I cooked a nice dinner of salad and fried trout with grits.

We had our fill of dinner, then took a stroll over to the video store so the lady could pick herself out a movie for us to watch on the houseboat. Though romantic French movies with subtitles weren't exactly my favorite, I knew if I behaved during the movie I'd have a good time later.

Later, after we'd thoroughly broke-in the new king-size bed, I lay there with Mary Ann asleep beside me and drifted off looking forward to the next day, and the rest of my life.

Acknowledgments

The book you hold in your hands would never have made it into its present form without the patient help of Annie, Sandra, Rebecca, Roger, and others from the Internet Writers Workshop. A special thank you to my family and friends for your encouragement and advice along the way.

Robert Tacoma is also the author of *Key Weird.* He lives in Central Florida and divides his time between working on his next novel and looking for his pets.